PEN SISTAS PUBLICATIONS

Tears Of A LONELY Child

LADII RAH

Tears of A Lonely Child
-Written By-
Ladii Rah

Copyright © 2020 by Pen Sistas Publications
Facebook: Author Dequonna Loatman
Instagram: LadyRah

Cover Design: Tina Louise
Editor: Tamyra L. Griffin

Table of Contents

Chapter One

5th Year: Just the Beginning

As young children, we are vulnerable. Fearfully learning ways of life's curiosity, we try not to make too many bad decisions or mistakes. We try to learn from relatives, friends, or in the most urban neighborhood on the streets; but what if we were born with no real options? What if a mother, who is genetically designed to nurture and love you, picks up and leaves you high and dry? At birth, this transformation can be damaging to youth. It leaves children emotionally and mentally unstable. Here's how my journey of disappointment, trust, and abandonment started.

At six months, I and my five siblings were taken by the state. My parents, both missing in action, we're out doing God knows what. Because I was only an infant, I could not possibly understand what was happening. We got thrown away like trash! What I can do is start from the day I do remember. I was five, about to turn six years old. I could remember waking up in the hospital with IVs and tubes in my nose. I remember Easter songs, and the ornaments hanging from the hospital ceiling. Opening my eyes, I recall seeing a yellow Easter Bunny in front of me. It was a tall, dark, slim man and a caramel-complexed small figured pretty young chick standing by my bed. The dark-skinned guy's name was Willis. He had a bit of a scruffy look. He was talking and whispering to the caramel, pretty young lady. His eyes were filled with tears and I heard him say, "Why would she take those pills?"

The caramel lady replied, "Mom said because she felt nobody loved her, and that they loved her sister more. So she climbed up on the shelf in the dining room and took twins' heart pills."

I can see the lady had tears in her eyes as well. Of course, I still couldn't understand what any of this meant, I was only a child of five years old. I just felt dizzy, nauseous, and had to throw up a lot.

Once I was discharged from the hospital, the same people that were in the room with me came with me to my grandmother's house. Once I got home it was explained to me that the dark-skinned man and the caramel woman were my birth parents, my mother and father. Even though I was still out of it due to the medication, I do remember how beautiful this lady was. She was about 5'5, big hips, big butt, nice lips, small waist, no stomach, shoulder-length hair, and she was dressed in all black jumper with red pumps. Beautiful. I could remember just looking at her, amazed the man looked to be rough looking. Maybe he'd just gotten off work; but hey, who was I to judge? So, that was my very first time seeing my birth mother. God knows I had no idea that the next time I would see her would be years later. Up until then I lived my life with my siblings and my grandparents.

My grandmother was a strict church goer by day, and a sinner by night. Her name was Ester. She loved Paul Mall cigarettes, and Pepsi soda. My grandfather Anthony wasn't much of a talker, but a more laid-back type of guy. He wasn't real loud. He was real militant, a hard worker, and he was always about his business. If you ask me, granny had a great man; one most would inspire to be. I could only remember him working and being involved with the family. My grandfather Anthony worked hard enough to afford a seven-bedroom house for his family. They also had a car, and all the basic necessities. Pop-pop was my best friend, up until he passed away when I turned ten years old. He had serval strokes, and with each stroke, his health seemed to deteriorate. After his first two he could no longer speak, walk, anything. All he could do was curse. Fuck; shit; bitch; asshole. I used to sit with him and color, then I'd put my pictures all over his wall. I couldn't go to Pop-pop for help, but just sitting with him was my escape - which is probably why I picked up the cursing habit. Guess it just stuck with me. A couple of months after the sexual abuse, he was extremely sick by then. It couldn't have been the worst timing.

I can't say I ever saw the family without lights or gas, food, etc. Ester and Anthony had seven children together - my three uncles, and four aunts. This house was always packed. There was always company, cooking, and loud music. People were always people around. My siblings and I were forced to clean up behind these nasty ass people. We were forced to wear hand-me-down clothes until someone important came over - then we had on new clothes and shoes. I mean now look, don't get me wrong. I'm not the only child that grew up in the eighties who wore hand me downs, but I felt things could have been different. I don't want to come off ungrateful, but some stuff I can't go on without speaking on.

I guess you can say we had the best hand me down clothes, and on the visits from the church folks and nurses, Granny made sure we looked our best if someone was to pop up. Granny wanted to make sure nobody would judge her. She felt like she had to prove a point and tried to save face in front the people. So of course my siblings and I were just not that important. I would never have thought to get me, and my siblings would be dressed in any of the attire we had; but I guess I wasn't cold or naked, so I was being taken care of in society's eyes.

We never really had any real love. There was always a hidden agenda for some weird reason. Behind it was a catch. With us being with Ester, she got over seven hundred dollars in stamps; and let's not mention how much cash she got for us. We were the real bankroll to this family. The thought I dealt with wondering about was if loving us was ever part of the plan. But I guess since they did take on a responsibility that was not theirs I have to respect it.

My mother thought given us to our grandparents was the best option so we would remain together. Honestly, being a mother while trying to shake a drug habit and the street life at the same time was a lot to take on. She did not want us in the system. She wanted us safe and secure until she could learn how to be a mother. She felt that we would be better off with Ester, and we'd still have each other; unlike my other three siblings who were adopted out to different families already, I couldn't tell you much about them. I believed my mother didn't want them to take us and adopt us like the state had done my other three siblings, but later on in life my birth mother would find out that the decision she made was one of the worst decisions she could have ever made.

When I was at the age of six, we were told that mom never loved us, nor did she want to see us That we were products of prostitution. She was a prostitute, always in and out of jail, and strung out on drugs on top of selling the drugs she didn't do. By the age of nine we were told that she had overdosed and passed away, leaving us with family. Basically I was born to a woman that I would never know or see besides that day at the hospital. I didn't know her, and there was really no chance of me ever getting to know her. Just the thought of my reality saddened me. Little did I know, my life was about to change severely.

A year and a half later after she'd passed, closer to me turning eleven years old, my body was forming. Things were happening to me that I didn't understand. I would come to resent who I was, and what I looked like. I was shaped more like a woman than a child, and I had an ass like Mama's. Body for days at ten, almost eleven, was a curse in my eyes. I guess that opened up the door for older guys, relatives, and family friends to try to give me strange attention, force me to do oral favorites or receive weird affection.

My twin aunts Kelly and Shelly were in their early twenties and had recently been allowed to start dating. From what I'd seen, things seemed to get serious. The twins were allowed to have company in the house, sleepovers and all, but only when granddad was at work cause he didn't play that. When he was gone that meant boyfriends can visit and stay the night. I hated when granddad worked third shift. Boy oh boy what a fucking mistake that was. I already had to deal with a bunch of dysfunctional motherfuckers; from drama, to fighting each other, yelling, screaming, and homosexual escapades. Things you didn't dare to speak about; because in a black household, what happened in the house, stayed in the house, and would never leave.

At almost eleven, our house was a mental prison for me. Half of the things I encountered at that age kids shouldn't have even been around, let alone experience.

I wanted to tell so much but was afraid to. The whole situation was stressful and draining on my little mind. I was in a house where all of these things were happening to me and I could not talk because of the rule what goes on in the house stays in the house. So I'm left with keeping everything a secret; staying quiet to save space so they wouldn't be judged. They never realized that little old me was ten years old. I had to deal with who was going to cry tears for that child who wasn't allowed to show emotion and had to bottle up everything that the world had thrown at her. Who speaks when these children have no voice? Who was going to protect that lonely child? Who did this child have to run to? What long-lasting effects would she have to endure having to deal with being molested, physically abused, and mental restrained?

There was drinking, drugs, and gay relationships going on in the house like any other day. Our household had a dark cloud over it. This house was where my innocence was stripped from me one of those lazy days Grandma Ester laid in bed watching her westerns, smoking her cigarettes and sipping Pepsi - never really leaving her bedroom but to yell, scream, enforce rules in the house, and to discipline us. I didn't know if she was just sick or just plain lazy, but this day she had put me on punishment for not doing my chores to her standards. She made me wash her feet, clip her toenails, and paint her nasty toes like a was a damn Chinese lade at the nail salon. Then she made me clean the kitchen like some child slave would be forced to do. She had me clipping her feet and shit, like I was a damn Chinese lady at the nail salon.

I was already going to get a beating for not doing my chores right the first time, but while I was doing them I was sexually molested by my Aunt Shelly's 24-year-old boyfriend. His name was Robbie. He would come to visit my aunt on a regular basis, but during his visit he would have sex with me downstairs when our Holy Roller grandma was busy gossiping on the telephone with her church friends. I really didn't know why she stayed in the room so much, with her lazy old ass; but for the most part she was always in her bed, so this gave Robbie time to do whatever he wanted to because honestly nobody really paid attention. Everybody lived their own lives, doing whatever they wanted to do. Robbie came downstairs making small talk, asking weird questions. Then he swiftly walked up to me and started grabbing and pulling on my clothes. He pulled me into the corner where the heater closet was, covered my mouth and started to whisper in my ear how grandma should treat me better. How he feels bad about me being beat all the time, and how I shouldn't have to clean up behind all those dirty people. All in one motion Robbie kissed me, then pulled me in closer to his body. By then his hands were in my panties under my nightgown. I froze. It felt weird. His hands were cold, hard, and so rough it hurt. It felt wrong as hell. I knew I was a child and things like this weren't supposed to be happening. He knew he was wrong, but he just kept rubbing his hard fingertips roughly in and out of my little vagina. I felt hot. I was spooked. All I could think was, "Could this be okay? Is this right? He's a grown man and I'm a little girl." By then he keeps going.

In a lightning fact motion he turns me around forcing me on all fours and I'm feeling something wet running down my leg. He jumped behind me, slowly sliding his manhood inside of me, covering my mouth with one hand and directing his penis with the other. He slowly enters me continuously, over and over again, getting his pleasure out of this. He's moaning softly but has a deep tone that makes it feel even more weird. I'm squirming, trying to yell; naturally because his manhood was too big and I'm a child. That shit hurt. He takes a few more pumps, jumps off of me, and says, "Don't tell anybody, it's our little secret. I will protect you." Robbie said he wouldn't allow anybody to hurt me. At least that's what Robbie had me to believe. I was scared and confused. I looked at Robbie, nodded yes, and after he kissed me he left the house. He comes back hours later like he just had got there, acting like he didn't just fuck me.

I ran to the bathroom to pee and wash the blood out of my panties and off my skin before someone came in and saw I was bleeding. Blood was everywhere. On the toilet seat, a little on the floor, and the toilet water was completely red. I grabbed as much toilet paper as possible and started trying to clean up the mess I made. Once I did that I put on one of the granny pads and headed back downstairs to finish my dishes. Afterward, my grandma came downstairs talking shit as usual while I thought to myself, *'Look lady, I don't have time for your shit today.'* I would never say this, just think it. She just came to see how far on the chores I had gotten. I wanted to say I really did not get anywhere cause Robbie's old ass was rubbing on me and fucking me granny, but no, I didn't say that either. There was a lot of shit I could not say.

I didn't get far so, that means I was getting my ass whooped. I see her coming downstairs with this old, pink flower gown on, which was tight and wrinkled, with a cigarette hanging out her mouth. She was a small, thick lady; and mean as hell. She walks in the kitchen, already trying to start something. She starts wiping her fingers across the dishes. Of course one of the pots had to have grease on it. She then hits me in the top of my head with the pan over and over until it broke and fell to the floor. She then grabbed a broom to finish me off, hitting me all over my body. I tried to block the hits on some Bruce Lee shit, you know, but by now she's going crazy with it. The first thought popped in my head was, *'Where is Robbie? He said he would protect me. Where is he at now?'* I'm alone again, as usual, and the worst part was I was getting my ass beat because of him. If he had not been touching on me I would have been done.

I just balled up on the floor and took that ass whooping as Grandma kept swinging while I tried to block her hits. She cut my arm open with the broken broomstick, so now I'm bleeding all over the place and I'm sitting here like why is this old lady trying to kill me? She grabs a damp kitchen towel and wrapped my arm with it. No hospital, no 911, not even Band-aids. At this point I'm trying to find ways to leave this house. At least it would stop the ass whoopings and the sexual abuse. But no matter how bloody, I was I still had to finish the kitchen. 10 years old and I'm feeling like she's trying to hurt me. She thinks I'm a damn slave child. I'm starting to understand I'm alone and need a plan. What happened to Robbie saving me with his lying ass when I needed him the most? I really have nobody. He lies like everybody else.

I finish doing my chores then went into the bathroom to take a bath. I was still bleeding from earlier and didn't want anybody to see it. When I got in the tub it burned so bad. My little vagina was feeling like I had gotten cut down there. Sitting in the tub, tears fell from my little eyes as I cried and prayed to God that I could get past this pain. I was even trying to pray to my deceased mother. I felt that I was that child nobody cared about and nobody would ever listen to. I was baffled and my mind was racing with so many thoughts; like this old ass lady really just was trying to do so much harm to me behind me not completing a chore. At that point in my ten-year-old life, I just didn't want to live anymore.

I went to my bedroom, took my grandfather's leather work belt, wrapped it around my neck, and put the metal buckle on the handle of my bed. I jumped from the top bunk hoping to break my neck. It was too much, and nobody ever cared. Nobody ever listened. I thought the idea would have worked. Instead I just fell to the floor and gagged slightly, but it didn't kill me. I took the belt from around my neck and cried as I went to finish washing old and new blood off me. Afterward I dried off, putt on my pajamas, and headed to bed.

Chapter Two

Who Cries for This Child?

The next day I was still sore and completely drained headed out to school to start the same routine. School, home, homework, and chores over and over. The next day I was still punished. I headed to the kitchen to do my chores. Nobody was in the house at the time, it was just me and my siblings. Everyone was still at work, and Granny was of course laid up. Then my aunt's other boyfriend comes in from work. His name was Wilbert. He walks in, saying he's going to wait on my aunt to get off from work. He then asks me where everyone was, then he says he's going to go speak to Ms. Pings; Ester's nickname, which was my grandmother's name. I started my dishes, then he comes back downstairs and into the kitchen. He started talking to me, asking me my name and how old I was. I go into the basement doorway to grab the broom and he follows me into the closet. He grabs me, and swift as Robbie he slides my pants and panties down, covers my mouth, then bends me over and enters me from the back. Pumping and pumping rapidly, he did his do, but he heard a noise and got scared. He furiously pulled his clothes up and ran off.

"Tell your aunt I stopped by to see her and I'll be back when she gets off work."

I just felt so disgusted trying to understand if I had 'Violate Me' stamped on my face. I felt like the older I got the more I understood; and who can I tell? Who can I go to that would really listen? Nobody, that's who.

Months went by, and still, no Robbie. I started to believe his ass got kind of scared and thought I was going to tell what he did to me. Honestly, it'd been so long since it happened, and nobody ever really noticed, so I just put it in the back of my mind and went about my life. I felt Robbie was the only one that I could confide in, so I thought I was in a relationship with him. At least that's what he had me to believe.

After about two months Robbie started coming back to visit. Sometimes he would come to bring me money, candy, and marijuana cause he was the weed man. I had that all the time, and it kind of started helping with all this mental pain. I started to self-medicate with beer, and liquor, and cigarettes every now and again, at ten years old, I was smoking weed and drinking. My life was spiraling out of control. I felt like a whole grown-ass woman. Shit, everybody was fucking me, I didn't see why I couldn't do it all. Like all the other grown women, it was my only out. The only time I felt safe was with Robbie. We still were having sex, but he was teaching me the game as he called it. Robbie taught me how to lick his nipples, which I thought was so gay, but he got aroused when I did this; and he'd teach me how to orally please him. He would give me oral as well.

Time went on, and the older I became, what he couldn't get from my aunt he would get from me. Our sex life became just that, our sex life. Probably by this age I am now, I started to experience feelings I really couldn't understand at twelve. I felt like he was mine, even though he was with my aunt and she had a child or two with him. I didn't know any better. Shit, I was a kid, I was just going with the flow. I had no other way to survive. I can't beat them, so why not join them.

I guess by twelve I was a pro at fucking, and at that time all I knew was to please him. I had just gotten my period, so now I was really feeling grown; and to Robbie, I was his P.Y.T (Pretty Young Thing). I was eye candy, 'cause my aunt wasn't the best looking lady. but she had a pure heart. Another year went by and I was getting wise beyond my years when I needed to say something. Plus after having my period for a year now, my body started to feel different. My breasts were filling out more, and my ass was bigger. I was grown just all the way around the board.

I want to say something because I was getting older and started to have my own view on the whole situation. I wanted to tell someone so I could get away. My only outing was school, and my counselor, Mrs. Royal. She was a Hispanic Jamaican lady with an awesome accent. She made me feel comfortable and safe in her presence. I went to school one morning, as usual, but only this morning I physically was feeling sick to my stomach and didn't know why. When I spoke with Ms. Royal, we discussed how I was feeling, and she made me get a check-up at the nurse's station. At this point I was called in for my results and I was pregnant. She gave me a card, told me to check in with a primary doctor for more test and better care. Of course she questioned me, told me the pros and cons, as well as my options about adoption. What was I going to do? I had to talk to someone, but who?

I knew I had to tell my sister Falisha about the things that were going on with me. She's a year older than me, and always considered the family favorite. We didn't really get along because she had a smart-ass mouth, but she was still my sister - and really all I had. I think I figured I'd tell her bits and pieces, because she would just blow it up if she knew it all. I at least needed her to know what my plans were and what I had been through. So I told her how both of our aunt's boyfriends were touching me and had been fucking me since I was nine. I told how I do drugs, drink, and smoke cigarettes. Then on top of all that I feel sick, my vagina burns, and itches so bad that I something's wrong with me. My sister hugs me and we cried together, but I knew the type of person she was - and I'll be damned, just off of that little bit of information Falisha goes and tells the family what we talked about. They called for a family meeting, and it was "mandatory". No if, and's, or but's. Straight like that. The moment I sat down I could see and feel the glares from everyone and they're expressions were filled with so many different emotions. Disappointment, anger, jealousy, and hatred. The tension in that room was so thick you could see the steam forming in the air, but I built myself up enough to have the courage to address the room and whatever came next. Of course, everyone came with the questions, so I came with the answers. I definitely let them know about how I've been sexually touched by Robbie and Willie. Not so much Willie, because he did it once and never did it again. I think maybe he was scared, or he just felt bad. It Robbie more so.

As I'm explaining the situation to everyone, my twin aunt Shelly, Robbie's baby mother, jumps up and charges at me - trying to fight me like I was the one in the wrong. I mean she literally chased me down the street with a board that had nails in it! She came for me like I was a chick from the block, and I ran like I was a track star trying to win a trophy. Afterward, we're back at the house and she's yelling stuff like, "Oh, you're a hot ass!". "You probably threw yourself at him.", "You probably like that!". "You're a liar! I'm gonna kill you!". She pretty much claimed she could keep count for every hour of his life. She was clearly in denial, but she knew his timing at each place, everywhere he had been, when he had gone, and apparently how long he took to return. She had an answer for everything. She protected this man with everything within her being, when she probably knew deep down that he wasn't shit, and he did all the shit I said he did. I'm sure she has seen the signs. The distance he kept her at when he was in the house. He was spending those lost hours with me and her children because she was working all the time. He was showing me the attention she wasn't getting, which had her wanting to fight me like somebody in the streets. That's not family. This is why I didn't say anything from the start, but I know why my sister went back and said something. When we spoke yesterday, she forgot to mention how Wilbert was fucking her like Robbie was fucking me - so it all made perfect sense now. Wilbert fucked me once, but Falisha was his main fuck. Shit's crazy, but I'm glad she spoke up, because I knew nobody was going to believe me. They would believe the golden child. so I figured I'd use Falisha as ammunition, and it worked.

It was out in the open, and they now knew everything. That I was pregnant, but not about STD. I knew my body was changing, and I was feeling sick all the time. I didn't want to say anything at nine years old. How was I supposed to know how to handle this, and that it really was not okay; but right now, you won't put this guilt on me. This man is grown. He violated me and you're trying to fight. The thought bewildered me.

I bolted out of that house and ran quickly down that street. I ran away from that family. From the brutal physical, sexual, emotional and mental abuse that came with it. As I'm running, I turn around to see Shelly running behind me with this big ass white wood board that she probably broke off from the front porch that was falling apart. Then I see Robbie coming out of nowhere, running behind her. He grabs her, trying to pull the board from her hands. Of course, seeing this shit had me mad.

I yell, "You're supposed to be over here with me. All this nonsense because of you! I just needed to get away from everybody. You said that you would protect me from all of this, and of course you're on the wrong side of the team!"

On top of that, I knew Robbie wasn't for me. Robbie made me out to look like a liar. Like I had just made all that shit up about him. So I knew he was fake. I knew how I had to play his ass from here on out. Robbie wasn't shit.

I just kept running, not even looking back anymore. There's no way I'm going back. Now I'm walking around not knowing what to do, or where to go. I guess I should have never said anything. Now I'm homeless and really have nobody. My father was in and out of jail, so who's going to protect me? I was going to protect me!! So I kept on walking until I found an abandoned house. I kicked the back window in and went into the bando. I found a blanket and a sheet in a bag in one of the downstairs closets. I'm sure it wasn't clean, but it was clean enough for me to get some sleep. I was mentally and physically drained. I didn't want to think about any of this. I didn't want to think about anything that happened. I just wanted to rest. It wasn't like I could think of any other sweet childhood memories. No way.

My head was spinning until I fell asleep. As time passed, I was suddenly awakened by someone lying next to me, trying to take off my pants. I open my eyes and Robbie was there trying to have sex with me. Everything was sex with him. I shook my head. He was always invading my personal space; and how did he even find me? I just closed my eyes back and let him finish. barely having any energy at all to put up a fight. I was bleeding all over.

He says, "Hold on, I'll be back. Don't move."

So I'm sitting in a blood puddle as he left. Shortly after he returning with pads, bottled water, and some snacks. He also brought napkins that I used to help clean me up. I put the pad on, and it felt like a diaper. I ate some of the snacks and drank some water. He went to speak, and before he could start talking I cut him dead off. I had a lot of things I needed to say to Robbie, and now was the perfect time. He thought I was that same naive ass kid. Nah, I needed to get some shit off my chest.

"First of all, you made me look like a liar in front of my family. That was foul." Of course he had an answer for that.

"I'm so sorry."

"Did you know that I'm also pregnant? Due December 12th."

He seemed a bit excited, then I brought up the STD he gave me. A fuckin sexually transmitted disease! Although I was pissed with him, I let him know that he needed to go get checked out. How dare he put me in harm's way? What if he gave me something I couldn't get rid of? I let him know right there that whatever we had, whatever it was - it is no longer. He played me for a fool. I felt like the child I was. I didn't know any better, and he took advantage of that; but the older I got, the wiser I had become. I learned a few things, and I learned that what he did to me wasn't right. He will be held accountable.

Once I told Robbie that I was done with this whole relationship he dropped on his knees and started crying, grabbing my legs, saying how he loves me. Begging me to please don't do this to him - as if he were not a part of the reason my life is ruined. He wasn't really my man. Robbie was just a pedophile, nothing more. He didn't care for me. It was that young, virgin pussy he loved, not me. He went on crying and pleading. He even claimed to have spoken to my family, and that they all were worried about me, wanting me back home. As much as I hated being there, I had nowhere else to go. I was dirty, needed a bath, tired, and hungry. I didn't want to be on the streets like this, so my dumb ass decided to go back home. I was numb to everything. I didn't make any of this shit up, yet Robbie and Wilbert made it seem like I was lying to save their asses.

Once I did get home, the atmosphere was awkward as hell. Everybody seemed quiet but somewhat apologetic. I did speak out on things, basically hoping it would stop, or something could be done; but no, I was wrong. It was all for nothing. Nothing was done about it - it was swept under the rug. It was never to be repeated, and never to be spoken of again.

Weeks had gone by, and still nothing had been done. By now I was feeling sick and throwing up. I'm eating more, and sleepy, but I still went to the school. When I talked to my guidance counselor I took a test a pregnancy test and it comes back I'm pregnant, which I already knew, and that I had a sexually transmitted disease. I knew that as well - I just didn't know the name of it. After this visit it was confirmed it was chlamydia, so that pain was just bacterial build up causing my lower abdomen to have pain. Talking further to my caseworker, not telling her anything too deep, I told her just enough to get to the doctors for medication and the things I needed for my baby. I couldn't tell these people in this house because then they would try to kill me. They would really be upset, and I would really be in the streets.

I can't tell anybody I just found out I was about five months pregnant. Then on top of that I was carrying an STD called chlamydia. Twelve and a half, pregnant and with chlamydia. I was scared and confused. I just knew I couldn't tell the family. They would just beat me and say I'm seeking attention, so I hid it up until I was eight months pregnant; but I needed to speak to Robbie. Does he even know what he gave me? The doctor said if I had waited any longer my child would have become blind due to not being treated. Yes I told Robbie he gave me something, but at the time didn't know the name. It was Terrifying.

At that point in my pregnancy, what could they really do? Nobody could do anything but listen - and being pregnant would stop the ass whooping. So I told my sister Felisha, and her snitch ass did just what I thought she was going to do, went and told. Then everybody goes crazy. The question of the day was of course, who was the baby's daddy? I told them I didn't know. My uncle, the gay one Lawrence who was the third boy child of Arthur and Ester, rushes towards me and attacks me - slapping me in my face. It happened in a flash, so I never saw it coming. He then takes his belt off on some Pooty Tang shit. Mind you this belt has these gold metal sharp spikes on it, and he starts swinging it wildly. I ran and got down in a corner and covered my belly. He just kept beating me with this belt all over my body. Trying to dodge his hits, I threw my arms up to protect me. All that did was get my arms cut up from all those hits. Cuts were up and down my arms, bleeding and in pain. All I thought was to protect my child.

My sister Felisha runs over and rushed Uncle Lawrence while screaming, "Stop, she's pregnant! You're going to hurt her baby!" She jumped on his neck, screaming, "She's pregnant! Stop hitting her!" So now she's getting jumped by two people, our grandma and uncle. It was at that very moment I knew that my sister truly loved me. We just had our differences. She put herself in the line of fire, and she was so much smaller than me, to protect me and my child. I just laid there in a corner balled up until this drama was over. Once I saw everybody was calming down, I got up and hauled ass for the front door. Yes, some may say I left my sister in there to get beat up, but I had to save myself. I ran and left her to save herself. Me and my baby had to go, we were in harm's way.

I had no shoes or coat on, in the cold and snow. I ran down the street about ten houses down my neighbor Miss Berta's. She hears me crying and screaming as I'm covered in blood. She yells, "Baby get over here right now. I got you." as she holds her shotgun in her hands. She was an old thug that drank and partied a lot but had a heart of gold. She was so sweet she took me in her house, cleaned me up, gave me a pair of shoes, a coat, and some clothes her daughters had laying around. She looked like a hood superhero with her shotgun. I explained to her some of what happened, and she called my uncle Ryan. He didn't live home. He was the productive, nice uncle who genuinely cared. He moved away and started his own family and was in college. He was the one with a great head on his shoulders, and he played pro football, so he was one of those uncles that was never home when he lived here. He was never in that house, so he was never a part of the chaos.

She explained to my uncle what happened, who then he assured her that he would pick me up and he thanked her for looking after me.

Uncle Ryan came and got me about twenty minutes later. I told him the truth - all the way from the beginning to end. He took me to the house and promised they would not hurt me anymore - he would make sure of it. So I did. I went back with Uncle Ryan and now he's calling his own personal family meeting. He's called everybody downstairs and allowed them time to get there. Everybody's running in a panic, because when Uncle Ryan, spoke you knew he meant business. They wanted to know what's going on, as if they didn't just attack me. Uncle Ryan expressed to them what they're doing to me is wrong, and that he knew everything. He also told them that instead of them blaming me, the child who really doesn't know right from wrong, we should be addressing the people that did the wrongdoing.

Uncle Ryan spoke with so much animosity in his voice. He was outraged and was determined to do something about it. He then asked his twin sisters where their boyfriends were and where they lived. My uncle wanted street justice - and had no plans to hand them over the cops. He wanted to fuck them up. He wanted to shoot some shit; take this shit back to the street for violating his favorite niece. Tears rolled down his eyes, so I know at that moment he could feel my pain and probably was embarrassed because it was his mother and his sisters.

Everybody acted dumbfounded, as if they didn't know what he was talking about. That was when he informed my aunts that when he saw Robbie he was going to beat him seconds from heaven, and Wilbert would not be able to walk again. He was in rare form.

Chapter Three

Praying for A Better Way

Uncle Ryan couldn't stress enough that if anybody were to put their hands on me again, they would have to answer to him. Needless to say I feel like somebody cares enough to stand up for me. Somebody hears my cry, finally. My uncle was going to protest for me to keep these people from abusing me, because this was wrong, and I was so tired of it. Then on top of that, I have a baby inside of me and all they were trying to do was physically harm me and the baby. I wanted out. I needed out. Until then, I'm just waiting to have my child. Waiting to speak with Robbie about our child and let him know I wasn't fucking him anymore. When I said it to him that day, I meant it with every bone in my body. I was just tired, and there were decisions I had to make. I had a baby coming into this world and an STD that I had to take care of myself, still thinking, what if Robbie would have given me something I could never get rid of?

I needed to talk to him, point blank, so I set up a meeting to talk to him in private at the southside park. When we met up I explained to him again that I was pregnant, and that he had given me an STD. I explained to him that I didn't feel comfortable with having sex with him anymore and that he needed to go get checked. Of course, he completely denied giving me anything. He basically insisted he didn't have anything, and that he would be there for our child. He kept trying to push everything I was saying to the side as if what I was saying didn't matter to him. Basically making it like he's older and knows more, while I'm younger and didn't know shit. That kind of pissed me off, so I went off again and repeated the same thing I said before. Whatever relationship we had going on, or whatever he wanted to call it, was no longer happening. I'm older now, and I realize that what we were doing was wrong.

I yelled to the top of lungs, "You robbed me of my childhood and took advantage of my vulnerability! I realize that he gave me drugs to suppress my reality, causing me to lose focus on the real world, and alcohol to numb the physical pain. To keep me stagnated; not to mention the cigarettes which were also wrong. You knew it was all wrong, so that makes you a different kind of evil." I spat as tears threatened to fall from my eyes. "I'm starting to see you for who you are. The rain has dried up, the skies are clear, and the sun is shining. I'm seeing things for what they really are now."

Robbie was a user, a joke, and a pedophile. Me talking with my mature twelve and a half-year-old mind, feeling like I'm turning twenty-five mentally, I let him know all I needed him to do was be there for our kid and left it at that. I believe that after that conversation he definitely looked at me differently.

My purpose in life was to wait for my baby to be born and try my best to be the mother that I never had. Now I'm just staying out of the way, living in the same dysfunctional house, and staying to myself - trying to avoid any negative energy. I didn't want to be stressed, and I didn't want to cause any complications for my baby. I believe my aunt Shelly had broken up with Robbie, and as karma would have it, she found out she was pregnant too. He would be faced with molesting me for the rest of his life, so can you imagine the niece and aunt pregnant by the same guy. Disgusting. I believe during the break-up with him, they decided to co-parent. I didn't really tell my family what I decided to do, and they still didn't know who my child's father was. I just let them believe whatever they wanted to believe. They actually had the audacity to say that I had multiple sex partners and didn't know who my baby dad was. That I was a little whore, along with every other name in the book. Little did they know I was a virgin before Wilbert and Robbie violated me and took my innocence, but I let them think what they wanted to. I've come to realize that these people are just crazy, and their reality is not everyone else's.

Since the day I had that conversation with Robbie about the sexually transmitted disease and our unborn child I hadn't spoken to him for a while, and I think it's best we kept it that way until my baby was born, and felt would need his father. Not saying I forgive him or believe what he has done wasn't right, but I felt if there was a chance of him being an okay father, I really didn't want to ruin that for my son; and not really having my father confirmed my thoughts. Robbie had to face what he did and be there for his son. Just when I thought things would settle down, things seemed to get worse. I left the park that day and headed home. To my surprise, I was met at the door by two guys - one older guy and the other younger.

Chapter Four

When Lies Come to The Surface

They seemed so genuine; and the crazy part about it is, the more I stared at them, the more I saw myself in them. We looked a lot alike. My birth mother had given them my address, told them I was being molested and pregnant, and wanted them to check on her children. She also wanted them to inform everyone she was in prison and would be coming home soon. All this seemed so strange to me, and all the information was a lot to take in at once. I had already been through so much, and just to hear all of this was even more strenuous. She wanted me to get to know them, and my birth mother wasn't dead?! That was all I could think of.

The strange look on my face told its own story. Why did they lie was my next question; and where had she been? All these years when I was going through all of this she was around. She was free, and she was alive. I was devastated. I could not understand what this man was saying to me.

"How are you my father? How is this guy my brother, and how is my mom alive when these people told me that my mother was deceased most of my life? Everything was a lie! My father ain't my father! This family ain't my family; and my mother is alive?!! What else don't I know?!"

After being told this, I went and told my grandma somebody was at the door after making sure I got all the information I needed before I was able to sit Ester down. The minute Ester saw who it was at the door, it was like she saw a ghost. A ghost from her past that came back to haunt her. She ran for the house phone and immediately called my Uncle Ryan screaming through the house phone to get here soon, and that there were two men on the steps as if they're there to do her harm. She really was being dramatic. She went crazy, started yelling and calling everyone downstairs to come to the door to come fight my real dad and my brother. They saw a herd of people running out the front door, and as soon as the older guy saw my older cousin with no shirt on he started pulling on the son, yelling, "Let's go son!" The son had a different view. He was like Scrappy Doo, ready to fuck shit up. The father was not with the shit and took off. They jumped in that car so fast, like the dad and the son in the movie Friday and burned rubber.

Technically nobody fought or anything, they just were talking shit, after all this time. Everything calmed down, this shit comes out, and I was definitely punished. I got some extra chores, but them ass whippings were out the door since they knew I was pregnant. They claimed none of that would have happened if I would have never answered the door. Clearly that was just them being narcissists, causing trouble yet never admitting it and throwing the blame. Somebody needs to take responsibility, and I guess I was the Fall Guy. I don't give a damn about all this extra cleaning. I do this all day anyway. I'm too numb. I'm so used to it by now; but I need answers, and I needed them now, so I went to grandma fearlessly. I'm pretty much ready for whatever. I knew it probably was going to cause an argument or some type of family feud, but I wanted to know, and I think I deserve that much.

She was off in her bedroom, inside the closet. I knocked on the door and she told me to come in. I sat her down calmly and unapologetic. She had this glare in her eyes, as if she were afraid to tell me the truth; but she knows that it has been exposed, so she had no other choice but to own up to this whole story. It was that moment every emotion hit me. I was angry, sad, lost and confused - all behind lies. My whole life was a lie.

"How could you lie? So Willie was not my dad?"

"He's you brother Zaheem and Felisha's father." she replied.

"Why did you lie to me and tell me my birth mother was dead?"

"Yes, Troy is your birth father. The father that raised you is your sister and brother's father. We couldn't find Troy at the time that your mother went to prison, so we took you in. Michael is your biological brother, your mother's oldest son. You also have an older sister. Chelle and your younger sister Temaki were put up in foster care with your mom and sister. She was two years old at the time. Michael was born a crack baby and was hospitalized for water on the brain, and a bad heart. He weighed 1pound, 1 ounce and wasn't supposed to live past six months. He wouldn't be able to speak, walk or function like normal kids his age because your mother was fourteen at the time the state took her and your older sibling to a foster home."

Rumor has it my brother had broken ribs and my mom couldn't take care of him. My sister she took the kids on the run, so nobody would take them from her, not really having any resources. When the state located my mother she was living in an abandoned car and it was snowing outside.

"It was one of the coldest winters in history. Because she was underage and the kids were neglected, all of them were put in placements. I'm shocked he is alive. I believe he was taken from your mother after that, so there was no way that you two could have been in contact.

Piecing my life together and learning new things, my voice cracks as the conversation continues.

"Now tell me why you lied to me? You said my mother died because she was a druggie and a prostitute when the whole time she was in town. Do you even understand what that has done to me mentally? "

She was always in and out of jail, so Ester claimed she did not want to get us all excited for her to not be in our lives. She claimed to do this as a way to protect me from being hurt. Little does she know to have her not tell me the truth hurts more, so it hurt me either way.

Her not being there hurt me. Her lying to me about having a dead mother hurt me, so who did she really save? I have dealt with so much pain, not knowing the truth and living a not so pretty lie. I'm pregnant, stressed to the max; too much to take in at once. I'm almost thirteen years old and my life has already gone up in smoke. Life as I knew it was no more, and by the end of me and Grandmother's conversation, I had all my answers. Now I know my birth mother was coming home soon and we can go live with her. Grandmother explained to me that my mother was in prison and had a ten-year sentence. She went down when we were younger, so her sentence was almost done. She was about to be paroled, and that meant we could go home. Grandma explained that someone's going to help her get housing, and that someone from family services was involved because she had completed parenting and all types of programs to be able to get us back. We can actually be with our birth mother now. The excitement of that was just all over the place! I was elevated. I mean, I get to meet my birth mother for the second time in a long time. This time I really can get to know her and see what a conversation with her would be like. It was an awesome feeling.

So now I'm pulling out the calendar and checking the days. October 10th couldn't come fast enough. I see how long we have, and I'm looking forward to meeting this woman again.

I hadn't seen my mother since I was five years old, and now I'm almost thirteen, and about to have my own baby soon. My mom was on her way, coming to rescue me. This was so much excitement for me. I believed everything was going great, turning around for the best. I believe that all those rough days I had endured, the dark clouds over my head… I believe everything was going to work itself out, because mama was coming home, and things would change. There wasn't going to be any more abuse, and no more homosexual stuff happening. The thought alone gave me a sigh of relief that my day was coming. Hopefully, it was about to change for the better, because living with Grandma, being molested, beaten like slaves and treated any kind of way was just tiring now.

Within weeks my siblings and I went on visits to the prison to visit my mother. Of course it was sad, and we all cried. We had our own questions, but she was more upset that her baby was pregnant than anything else. Her exact words were, "My baby is having a baby.", and I was stunned; but I was in my own thoughts of happiness at the moment. Just looking at my mother's caramel skin complexion, and those big, beautiful eyes, she was about 5'5 with full wide hips and the most beautiful smile a person could have. She looks just like my sister Falisha - or my sister looked just like her, except Falisha was darker; but she was everything I thought she would be. She was wonderful and had an awesome sense of humor. She had me and my siblings laughing the whole visit, even through all that pain and tears. I couldn't wait 'til we were able to be home together.

I hated having to leave my mother after visiting, just to go back to that house of torment, lies, and hell. Well, at least I was counting down the days until we could be together with her. In a twist in fate, which was about a month or so later, my mother was released. I was about thirty-six weeks, almost due, so that was pretty exciting because she made it in time to see me have my first baby. You can say that was a good thing, but it was perfect timing. My mother, who didn't show me how to be a mother, now can enjoy the highlights of being a grandmother. She pretty much missed all those things with us, and now she can show me things about parenting that I didn't even think she knew because she never was around then. She didn't raise any kids, so how does she know all these things; but I'll still listen and take heed.

Right now I wasn't trying to focus too hard on any of that. Mom had just got out and we were waiting on the car to head on over to meet her at the Department of Youth and Family Services. See the plan was to meet Mommy there, go pick up our keys and head over to our new apartment. Once we were there they had to speak to the family about assessments, and what was expected of my mother while she was on parole, different plans she had for her children, and what plans she had for herself. We were all involved in this conversation. We had to attend different counseling sessions, and she pretty much had an understanding of what she wanted to do; all with the mind-set of reforming her lifestyle. For her, that was her main goal.

We were home with Mom, and that's all that mattered. We had our first apartment and it was our first night together. It was like a dream come true. I was so happy. We all were happy. Shit, finally me, all my siblings and our mother were all together. Mommy cooked us dinner: chicken, macaroni and cheese, cornbread; and she made this Kool-Aid that was so sweet it made you tremble after the first sip.

We popped in a VCR tape, ate, laughed, and watched movies all night. The next morning when my siblings went to school, Mommy wanted to talk to me. I wasn't in school because I was due in a few days, and I knew it was coming. I knew it was about my son and my son's father.

"What happened?" she asked.

I didn't really want to talk about that before, but I believe now was the time. Time to tell my real mother what really happened to me. This conversation was well overdue and much needed; and I had questions that I needed her to answer for me, so I told my mother the full story. No lies, no hidden agenda, and no secrets. My mother cried, said she was calling the cops and was pressing charges and he would be charged; because how could he do that? How could they allow him to do that and nothing happened to Robbie?

Off we went out the door, and Mama did exactly what she said she was going to do. She dragged me down to the police station and she pressed charges against Robbie for molesting me. He was charged with molesting a minor, giving me drugs, and a few other charges. Afterwards we went back home, and she signed me back up in school. It was homeschooling of course, until I was able to attend regular school again. I got into a program for counseling and help with my baby. They gave me all this new baby stuff: a crib, bottles. diapers, and so forth. Things I would need to take care of my child. I would speak to my therapist maybe twice a week, just preparing me for birth on December third.

A few weeks after turning thirteen, I was admitted into the hospital. I was forty weeks, well overdue, and it was time for my son to come into this world. My doctor scheduled me to have my labor induced, meaning since he wouldn't come, they had to force him to come out. Stubborn ass baby. He's supposed to have been out two weeks ago. So, I get to the hospital for my scheduled appointment and I'm preparing for labor. They're giving me IV's and preparing everything needed. My mother is there, the father that raised me is there, no signs of my biological father, but one of my guy best friends Henry was there as well. Henry is physically handicapped, but he's so nice and he had the biggest crush on me. I didn't really like him like that, but I always kept him as my friend. Everybody was there showing their concern for me. I was in this hospital room for about ten hours in labor, no baby yet, and in excruciating pain.

I was a child having a child, maybe eight hours after the ten hours. I finally dilated to about four cm when I started screaming, "The baby is ripping me!" He ripped me from my booty to my vagina. Do you hear me? I'm screaming he's ripping me, and the doctor told me to stop pushing, but I continue to push anyway. I needed this baby out of me. I couldn't understand this pain.

"Get him out of me!" I yelled.

With one push and a loud scream I ripped completely open and a baby fell out on the bed. The doctor told me to be still, and that he was stitching me back up. I was completely ripped open. My vagina was ripped wide open, so it looks like I had no butt hole, just one big ass hole. Now I have to go through more pain to get stitched. Lord Jesus help me. I'm holding my mother's hand, and I had my dad that raised me in a headlock, but I had a family now. I had two people that I knew loved me unconditionally, and they were here to support me through this time. Even my school counselor sent pampers and thousands of dollars' worth of supplies to help. My son had a crib that turned into a table and desk on top of a full bed. This woman made sure he wanted for nothing. Honestly, he would be good for the first five years. That's how much stuff my school helped me with.

After the Storm, there's always a rainbow. My son was my rainbow. Born at 4:32 pm that night, he weighed about 6 lb. 8 oz. He was 23 and 1/2 inches long and had no complications. He was a pretty healthy child. He was so flawless, so adorable, my very own child. Someone who really will love me back. I named him Qadir Shleak, which means (one who is capable and powerful). A blessing out of the dark.

In seconds I found myself being a teen mother still learning. I thought my mom would do most of the work because I was a kid, and I didn't know any better. She helped do most of the work, but I needed to know what being a kid felt like. I didn't really want to be tied down in the house. I wanted to go play with my friends. Having a baby didn't make any of that possible, so I was forced to be a mother at thirteen. My mother had a different plan, she made me take care of my son. I'm not about to lie, I was tight. I had animosity because I had no childhood. Thinking that because I was back home with mom that she would allow me to have some freedom, I was sadly mistaken. The reality of it was, I was a mother and had responsibilities.

Chapter Five

Where Did My Childhood Go?!

I was so angry because I felt she just didn't want me to go jump rope with friends. Shit, I even wanted to smoke a Dutch, but because Robbie wasn't around I couldn't get weed or beer. My mom wanted me to take care of my son, which I didn't understand it at all. I wanted freedom, and I felt I was owed that. I was just locked up in this house with people abusing me, and now to come here I have to be a mom. You gotta be kidding me!! It felt like jail. I tried to be a mother, but Mom just screamed and yelled all the time at my indiscretions. Nothing was ever done right. Even though she had custody, I still tried my best.

Finally it was back to school for me. That's where I got most of my freedom. I needed to meet friends, be around people my age. I started hanging out and skipping school, just so I could get some free time. By then I'm already sexually active and having sex with different boys. Not really knowing my way, just doing whatever felt right to me. Trying to fit in. Trying to find my spot in life; so who would have thought. Maybe a year later I find myself pregnant again. Damn, I should have listened to my mom when she wanted me to stay home. All that lecturing went in one ear and out the other. She told me to sit my ass down and take care of my son. Now how was I supposed to explain this to her. Because I didn't listen, now I'm pregnant again at I'm fifteen and a half, with two kids.

I was never home, so my mom didn't know anything yet. She pages me 911 on the two-way pagers we had at the time, and of course, I called back.

"Yes Mom." I replied.

"Come home, your son wants to see you."

At this point, I had been away from the house for weeks. I hadn't seen my son in about two weeks. I was staying over different friend's houses, just drinking, drugging, and being grown. At fifteen years old, doing all of this stuff, I was out of control.

I said, "I'll be there.", and hung up the phone.

Once I got to my mother's house to see my son, my mother had already cooked dinner, so you know we sit down to eat, conversated, and out of the blue I just dropped the bomb on her.

"I'm pregnant again."

She looks at me with dissatisfaction before she starts screaming, and cursing. She's fussed for about two more hours. She's like who, what, why, how; and of course, who's the dad? So I told her it was this guy Twan from around the corner. Now mind you, he was a brown skin brother. He had these big old dimples, cute juicy lips, and pretty teeth with long braids. He was scamming credit cards and checks. He was the man, or at least I thought so.

She was like, "Yeah, I believe I know him.", and she got even more upset. "I believe that's my godson."

She's trying to explain all these different people to me, but I'm sitting here puzzled like, *'I just slept with my godbrother?'* How the hell was he my mother's godson? That wasn't the half. He was fucking my sister too! My mouth just drops open. Just my luck. I swear this shit seemed unreal, because at that very moment guess who walks in, hand in hand - my Sister and Twan. She was grabbing all over his arms as if they were in love. Now mind you, I was never home to see this shit or even kick it with my sister, so how would I have known this shit? Twan's greasy ass didn't say anything, and why would he? He knew I have been away from home for a very long time and wouldn't know who was screwing who. Grimy ass negro, sleeping with my sister Falisha at the same time as he was sleeping with me. So of course when I told my mom who this guy was she of course told my sister. Mom put it out on front street. Now mom was very outspoken; never holding any punches when she spoke about something serious. She was raw! There's no other way to say it. My sister and I started going back and forth, arguing over this guy. That's where I draw the fucking line. The dick wasn't even that serious, that shit was basic.

I sat there looking like the bad guy, and I'm like whatever. I tried to walk away and defuse the situation, but needless to say, we ended up getting physical anyway because Falisha knows how to push my buttons. She kept going and going, then started adding insults to injury. She started throwing fat jokes around, trying to show off for this boy. I wasn't about to let her come at me crazy, and my mom was just allowing her to get her shit off. We fought and I busted her ass, simple as that, right in front of Twan, Mom broke it up after a while. After all, I was pregnant; and came to find out my sibling was pregnant as well. So now we're both pregnant by the same guy. This can't be life. Fifteen years old, and pregnant by a nineteen-year-old boy that also has my sister pregnant. How the hell was she even talking to the same guy? We hung around different groups of people, but the shit happened and now I felt weird as hell. I left my mom's house and went to a friend's house. I really had no energy to sit around Falisha and Twan.

Monday I came home from school because I was trying to keep seeing my son regularly now. When I walk-in I noticed my sister was on the phone, so I told her when she was done I would need it. All extra, she rolled her eyes and said okay. I said okay and walked off. She was always trying to be sarcastic, saying she was going to be on for a while. Mom always made us share, and because we fight we have set times for the phone, like the county jail. I let her know I needed the phone so when she was done let me know. Her response again was, okay. I went to watch tv with my son. An hour went by, then another. I picked the other phone up to see if she was done. I needed to make a call. She went off, acting like I was sneaking trying to listen to his and her conversation. I wasn't just about to use the phone and was seeing how long she was going to be, so I walked in my bedroom. I didn't know if it was going to be a quick call or whatever, but I wasn't trying to be nosey. She just happened to be there two hours later. So now Falisha is off the phone cursing and yelling all in my face.

"You need to back up. You too close to my face." Me being petty I threw in, "Don't be mad I'm still messing with your boyfriend."

"I don't care. I'm pregnant and keeping it."

"Well I guess we both will be having his child."

This was out of hand, and she was in a competition by herself.

I'm supposed to do what again? I don't really know what reaction she wanted from me, but I really didn't care about anything she was saying. I'm keeping mine as well. I was all of three weeks further than her, which meant she purposely got pregnant - always competing with me. When I told her that, I turned around and walked away from her, trying not to feed the situation since I saw where it was headed. Then she fucking hits me with the phone in my head. From there we locked horns as she yelled how she was going to kill my baby. All this nut shit. I wasn't about to let her get away with hitting me. That was out. Like a raging bull, I went crazy. She had me mad as hell, so we just got right; pulling hair, punching, throwing each other around. I pinned her on the bed with her face in the mattress, told her to calm down, and if she stops I would let her off the bed. Of course she was still popping shit, but humbly agreed. She is sneaky and likes waiting till I walk away to hit me, so I really didn't believe her, but I let her up anyway. When I got off her to walk away again, she jumps on my back. I sling her ass across the room, she hit the floor hard and I jumped on top of her ass, punching her all in her head. Everywhere she tried to squirm I was on her. In the midst of the scuffle we knocked over the ironing board and the damn iron. Mom must have forgotten to unplug it before she left because that bitch was burning hot. When it fell it burned Falisha, but I didn't care. I kept whooping that ass till she begged me to stop. She was bleeding all over my mom's two-bedroom apartment. Yes, I did. I had thrown her ass all across the room. We were tearing that little apartment up. She's bleeding, I'm bleeding, hair was all over the floor. We even trashed my mom and Stepdad's room.

We went at it until my mom and stepdad got home. They had to break us apart, and of course my mom called me the aggressor. course. We both know it was more to this story, like I never did my chores or made curfew - and Falisha and I were always fighting, so I think my mom saw me as the source to the drama. I was the black sheep, and at the moment I just didn't care. I was frustrated and honestly tired of trying to please people. Mom told me to take a walk, but take a walk was always get out don't come back type of walk, so half the time I stayed outside. My mom cursed me out about it later that night when I came back. Why do we have to discuss everything we discussed earlier before I left? I don't need to see the need for it because nobody listens to me anyway. They always take sides. You know everybody has their favorite. I don't see a point in it, but I still fake listen to what she was saying. You know - that pump fake.

My sister was complaining of pain all that night. I'm thinking, *'Here we go. She always wants attention.'* My mother took her to the hospital. Come to find out, my sister's baby was inside her tubes and had erupted. She needed immediate medical attention because she had internal bleeding. Damn, this could result in her death. My mother was instructed to stay with Falisha as she would be admitted to fast-tracked surgery. She was losing blood and the baby was about to die. They rushed Falisha in, and she needed a blood transfusion. She felt weak, and soon after that she flatlined, but they brought her back and were able to keep her vitals stable. I'm stressed out the fuck out, sitting home feeling dumb as hell. I was crushed and my heart was in my stomach. I dropped down to my knees and cried out to God, begging for him to bring my sister through. This couldn't be happening.. I'm thinking all of this is because of me and this fuck nigga because that's exactly what he is. I didn't even know they were messing around.

As I was home stressing and pacing the floor the phone rang. My mother let me know by the grace of God my sister made it through, but her baby did not survive. I cried, thanked God, and felt sad all at the same time. Thinking and feeling like I had caused so much unnecessary drama. This is just too much to deal with. I felt so bad here. I was still pregnant by her boyfriend, and too far along to get rid of it, but her child was gone. I felt like a monster. Mom stayed at the hospital until they were able to get Falisha back healthy. The bad news is the doctor diagnosed her with Lupus. They learned this not long after everything. Damn, she is sixteen years old, lost her baby, almost died herself, has Lupus, and needed to get a blood transfusion. This was a lot to handle at the age of sixteen.

Mom spent a lot of time with her day and night at the hospital. I was stuck to fend for myself, learning to just do things on my own. Mom left me with my step pops and my son, on top of being pregnant again. I had no clue how to fully be a parent when I was young.

My sixteenth birthday was approaching, and again I was starting to feel alone in the world. My mother was so wrapped up with my sister that she didn't realize that I needed her as well. I needed her to teach me things, things that come from a mother; and to be honest, it was the same stuff she tried to teach me when I had my first son. Had I listened I wouldn't need her help. Instead, I felt unnoticed all over again. Once Falisha made it home from the hospital it got even worse. It felt like she was favored all over again, and these familiar feelings were something that I didn't want to relive. This wasn't love, and this once again didn't feel like family, so I just picked up and left. I needed to start finding my own way. I wasn't even noticed, so why would I want to be around. At that point, I decided to make a life for myself. A family. One that didn't know my past and just cared for me regardless; and that family was the streets. At fifteen years old, smoking, drinking, and fighting was what I knew best. I started gang bangin' and doing all types of craziness; but I felt noticed, and I felt like I was finally getting heard. When I would go home from time to time Mom was always yelling and trying to fight me for running the streets, not going to school, and barely seeing my son. So of course you know I ran off again. I couldn't take much of the animosity or the hostile environment, and I definitely wasn't. I left my son with my mom and didn't come back for a while. Two months later I'm back, and of course home and everything was calm for the moment; but that was the normal routine.

Chapter Six

Pick and Choose

My birthday and my sister's birthday were two weeks apart, and this is how I knew that love was different. It was my sister's birthday and she was turning seventeen. My mom and I went out and bought her boots, clothes, jewelry, and a birthday cake. I mean we did all of this stuff for my sister's birthday. She had to have the best birthday ever after all the hell she just went through. I thought that with me helping it would make everything all better again, and of course, we had an awesome time. We really turned up. Two weeks later it was my turn and I was so excited about the turn up that was about to go down. I waited patiently for my mom and sister to get home. When they finally did, you'll never guess what they got me. Wait for it, wait for it… nothing! Absolutely nothing at all. She told me a happy birthday.

"I'm broke because I spent everything on your sister two weeks ago, so you have to wait 'til my next paycheck comes, which is on the first of the month." Mom explained. My sister sat there unphased at what she was saying.

"So how is it she got something for her birthday, and I got nothing? I'm younger." Once again I am left with nothing. "Okay, I see everybody has a favorite."

That's the way I take it. It might not have been meant like that, but that's the way it seems. There were even times when I would come home when I was living in the city and would get blamed for stuff that Falisha did. I wouldn't say nothing and just take the L. One day I came to the house and the house is dirty. It was like my mom had been on a drug binge for several days, and my mother was pretty clean on a normal day. You could eat off her floors; but on this day when I arrived it was a mess. I fell asleep on the couch, because I was tired, and I woke up to a switchblade to my throat. I blink to clear my vision and noticed that it was my mother holding a blade to my throat, screaming, and yelling how her house is dirty.

"Why would I leave it this way that way? If you gone bad mouth me, go ahead and kill me already. Other than that, let me up off the couch."

I had to let her know that police had been here all day and she lives here. I told her I was just getting there and was always trying to be accepted. I just went with it and cleaned up.

"Clean up? How could you?!"

The more I objected, the harder she pressed down on my throat. I was shocked. I was afraid. I was saddened; but it explains again how Falisha's her damn favorite. I'm pretty much tired of the favoritism shit. I matter, like black lives matter, and everything just seemed to come out at once as I'm remembering all this stuff playing in my head. How many times my mother had taken Falisha's side. I just went crazy. Verbalizing how I felt, I yelled out, "I can't tell you the last time I even got a gift. My birthday just wasn't important!"

After that day I left and signed my pregnant self into a teen shelter. I needed to better myself, show my mother and my son I was worth something, and that I could right my wrongs. This place was going to change my life in some major ways. They can help me with school, getting my own place, my license, and getting a job. I could be a regular law-abiding citizen far away from the life I knew.

Chapter Seven

One Step Forward, Two Steps Back

I wanted more. This lifestyle was not it. I felt like I needed help, and I had to start somewhere. I wasn't afraid to ask for help. I'll call Qadir and check in on him, but I wasn't going back though. That whole situation was my last straw, but I would definitely check on everybody. My mother would call with concerns and beg me to come home, but I couldn't. I needed to find me. I needed my own space, and I didn't feel loved. I know how being unwanted felt. I wasn't wanted there, and I didn't want to be somewhere I felt unloved. Of course, after all the begging and crying she did, I eventually went back to visit because she sounded so worried. I didn't say I was going to stay, but I promised I would go to visit. I guess that made her happy enough, so I went with that.

When I got to my mom's house I stayed longer than I expected. The visit was okay, but things still seemed off with me and Falisha, I guess you can't fake everything. Some shit just ain't real. Regardless, she was still her favorite and I was still invisible, but I stayed around for a minute. Meanwhile, mom was still on parole and still with my stepfather, but she was having problems of her own. My stepdad was lying and cheating, which led Mom to start drinking again.

"Mom, you've been sober and drug-free all this time now your back drinking?"

"I can hear everything happening, but I just chose to zone out of it; you know, the arguments and the fights that continue, knowing that one triggers the other? Yep - and right now I don't give a fuck!"

Once she responded like that I knew where this was headed. I started to feel like that lost child nobody loved, as I would never be good enough because all the things I had been through things that were meant to break me. I had to stay strong, even on days I really didn't feel like it, because I was protecting myself. I had built up a shield, this safe haven around myself to be able to cope. It was like I was there, but I wasn't there. My energy was enduring all that life had thrown at me; but this one day my step pops and moms got into a really big argument. You could tell she had been drinking because she was in beast mode all day, and her beast mode was reckless. She takes his keys, storms out the apartment, and squeals off in his Bronco work truck. Already drunk as hell and driving, a recipe for disaster!

Hours go by and moms still out running crazy. Now I'm worried, calling around trying to locate her. My stepdad had been left on foot trying to find her and cursing the whole way out the door about his fuckin truck; but what happens next isn't funny at all. Come to find out mom blacked while she was driving, flipped the truck a few times and was still knocked out by the time the cops arrived. By the grace of God, no one got hurt behind her recklessness and she walked away with just a few scratches and a broken ankle. What she didn't walk away from was the violation of parole she'd just caught. She wasn't supposed to be driving let alone driving drunk. Needless to say, she was in the hospital handcuffed to the bed, reeking of booze with a handful of reckless driving charges by her side; and right after the doctor got the cast on her ankle the cops hauled her off to the county jail. Damn mom, back to square one.

God knows how long I'll be stuck at the apartment with my stepfather, sister Falisha and my son before mom comes home this time. This shit seemed all too familiar. Now from where I stand it seemed to be that Falisha and our stepdad we're having some type of sexual relationship on the low. When Mom went to jail my step pops was left to take care of my sister and I guess they started the bull, but I couldn't tell mom cause that was her favorite child and she really won't believe me; and we all know I was looked at like the trouble maker the child that just wanted attention. How would I know this was happening? First it was the signs, then I walked in on them before, and experience; because I know the times I was sexually touched by a man before, so it all seems too familiar. I know my mother knew nothing about this situation because she was in jail, so I just kept it all to myself. I know one thing though, that stepdad shit was out the window from this point on I will refer to him as Garite.

My mother had to finish two weeks of jail, then she would be released and back home with the family. Then things would change.

Five weeks from having my second son I needed to come up with a plan. This home is way too dysfunctional, and I can't go on like nothing ever happened; especially when everything is being blamed on me. All because Falisha and I carried a baby by the same guy I knew what the real hate was about, and my mother is blind to what's really going on; but shit, I'm always the blame is what I hear. I just need to figure out my life. There's always something different that pops up, and it's always some drama. I never have time to think my thoughts through, but not this time. I sat my ass down with a piece of paper and a pen and wrote down a few things that I needed to do to figure things out for myself. The school was so far in my past that it wasn't even a choice, so next was giving my son to a relative until I was eighteen. As long as I'm be able to come back and get them, I was fine with that. By then I should have a job and my own place.

I asked my cousin Marlene to take my second son. She was a cousin on my mother's side, but she was always helping the family out with their kids. She even has my brother. Marlene was the best choice that I had to work with, so I met up with her at a McDonald's in Atlantic City. We talked about my plans and she was on board. Marlene stayed in contact with me until I gave birth.

After my labor we stayed in the hospital for days. I called Marlene and she was right there to pick us up. That day was the hardest day of my life. I had to leave my baby for a while to better myself and get my life on track. I was heartbroken, I was leaving another one of my children with a family member. I felt like it was a cycle jumping from generation to generation. I wonder is this what my mother felt like when she gave us to whomever.

After that, I packed a big bag of clothes for myself and headed to my new boo's house.

Chapter Eight

The Journey to Find A Way

The Infamous Patrick Miller. He was this short, dark skin brother that had all these muscles, lots of tattoos, and perfect lips. He was my boyfriend and was willing to help me get myself back on track, so that's where I'll be living. He sold drugs and had a few other hustles going on. I think I was about sixteen and a half, and he was my only source of getting away from things. He had an apartment that he rented from this dope fiend and being as though the guy was never home, he told me I could come and stay with him. I was excited, and now I don't have to depend on my mom. I went to his apartment and when I walked up he was outside with no shirt on. His skin was a beautiful, smooth chocolate and he was steady smiling all hard with his pretty teeth. He was my world, and I loved me some Patrick. I thought he loved me too.

A year in and we're still going strong. He taught me the game, point blank period. He told me bag 'em, weigh 'em and stash 'em. Even though he knew I was street, he taught me more about the streets. He felt there was some shit I still needed to learn. He was always teaching me new sex positions and all types of kinky shit, I even experienced anal for the first time, but by then I was pretty much a pro. Outside of all the street and freaky shit, he also taught me how to be productive as well. I spent day and night with him for the next year and a half. We were young and in love.

On my 18th birthday, Patrick had bought me a car. It wasn't a Benz, but it was mine. He got me a 1999 Mazda 626 to top it off. I had just moved into my first apartment, so you know I was gassed. I worked two jobs, one at a factory called Leones glass in Bridgeton - packing boxes and checking glass for defaults. It was always hot as hell in that factory, but I was on my grind. What life taught me so far is nothing is for free and nobody owes you nothing. You don't work, you don't eat. I was so proud of myself. My other job was telemarketing at Hardy Hanks. There I would just call people and try to sell them things over the phone. Either way, it was paying my way and it was a layup. Both jobs were helping me maintain my lifestyle, and my bills. From where I just came from I could say that my life was pretty good, and I was proud of what I was building, with the help of Patrick of course. I was good, or so I thought.

Another year went by and I'm still just living it up. Working, grinding, partying - still being young, dumb and free. Just enjoying life, feeling like I was healing. The more balance, the more I felt the growth. Things were moving so fast, but hey, I was happy for the moment. For a second in my lifetime I could actually breathe easy and I was enjoying it. I went to go visit both my boys. Qadir was three now, and Adonis was turning two. They were also coming to visit for the weekend. I had to arrange it that way because I worked all week, and the weekends were the only time I could spend with them. I know it wasn't much, but I was making an effort, and it was a step towards me being a fulltime mother.

When I went back to visit my oldest son, I knew I had to have this conversation. I knew my mother would probably not agree, but these were my children and my plan were to grow and come back for my son. I mentioned I wanted to bring my son home for good. Of course, my mother objected to that and said if I took Quaidr it would kill her! She was too attached, and he was too. It would hurt him as well. I couldn't really understand it. I thought she was trying to strip me from being a mother then. I wanted to be his mother full time since I was eighteen and everything was looking up for me. I wanted my son home with me, and I explained it to her.

"Look Mom, my plan was to better myself and come back for my children. Now I have my own place, a job, and now I'm coming back for my children." Something my mother never did until we were almost grown with kids.

So now she's trying to strip me from being a mother. I was ready and able to be there the right way now, and she just kept saying no. I felt so disappointed, discouraged, and empty. I felt like all the progress I've made was for nothing, and I was doing this for them. I haven't had a drink in a year. I wanted to have a drink, I needed to have one, so I called my boo Patrick and told him I was going to the liquor store. I need a pint of strawberry Mad Dog and a twelve-pack of Colt forty-five. The ones that came in the can.

"Say no more." he told me. "I got you; just met me at the dope spot."

Chapter Nine

I Need A Break, A Change in Fate

Once I got there, I sat and had a drink with the lady of the house. Her name was Terry; an older black lady who would cook and feed the hood, but she got high and was a drinker. She was alright with me though, and she would share things with me well beyond my years of growth. I wasn't worried about the rest of the chicks around because I don't do bitches no way, so I was always drawn to hanging with older women.

Patrick was in the room with the other dealers rapping, playing video games, and drinking. He was my dude, so I was there with him just trying to ease my mind, drinking my drink. I get up to go in the living room to ask for a cigarette, and all of a sudden he starts getting smart and shit. Now I don't know was it all the shit I've been through that made me black, but he said a few words and I cut his ass up I snapped. I felt he was trying to show off in front of all these dudes, so of course, we started arguing. He began talking about how he needs another bitch in his life. Now don't judge me, judge your momma. He was singing a Biggie song at that point, and I snapped.

"Bitch, I just did a five-year bid with you and you're talking about another bitch!" I was so frustrated I walked in the kitchen and grabbed the biggest knife that I could find. I walked back in there and yelled, "You want to show the fuck off and disrespect me?! Here's your other bitch!", and I stabbed him right in his hip.

I went to swing the knife again at his face, barely missing my target. He jumps up screaming in pain, "She stabbed me! She stabbed me!" I didn't say shit. I just had that crazy look on my face like a hurt woman out for blood. I looked down at the knife and only seen half of it covered in blood. The other half most have broken off in his hip bone. I didn't give a fuck. I threw the rest of the knife at him and walked out, leaving him bleeding everywhere. Not a tear fell from my eyes, as I was clearly drunk out of my mind. Two seconds later I fell on the ground crying, now realizing what I did. I just stabbed the love of my life, and I'm super drunk. My drunk ass ended up calling the cops, telling them that Patrick was selling drugs and he has weapons. I also said that he put his hands on me so that he could go to jail. I was mad as a motherfucker. He said he needed another bitch, so I was showing him another bitch. All jokes aside, I just felt rejected again - feeling not good enough. He was doing to me what everyone in my life had done. Could that be the reason why I did it, or was I just a jealous young girl? I really feel like both played a part.

I pride myself in being real, and felt I was always trying to be enough in all aspects of life, not just in relationships. How dare this clown disrespect me after all the time, effort, and love I gave him. I mean, I gave this man all of me, just for him to turn around and pull this stunt. Fuck that and fuck him were my thoughts; but my raging, bull headed ass never thought of the consequences, nor a jail cell. I just sat on the curb drunk, throwing up waiting for twelve to pull up so I can really make a scene. When twelve pulled up, I laid down and showed out. I mean I was really putting on a show. Something clicked in my head and I jumped up to run off.

The damn cop yelled out, "Excuse me ma'am, you're going to jail right along with Mr. Patrick. I see you were trying to run you but failed to mention that you stabbed that man. You forgot to tell us that part."

I looked up and one cop was parked by me. They already had Patrick in the car. I could see his face and he was pissed, but he still tried to mouth to me how he still loves me and isn't pressing charges. I'd just turned eighteen, got my own place, a car, and I'm about to lose everything. I just work so hard for Patrick, but what was done was done.

All I remembered was waking up in the county jail the next morning sick. I was on the list to see the judge, and of course they called the Department of Children and Family Services because I was still a ward of the state. Even though I didn't live home with my mother, I was still state property. That label still stuck with me, even after being eighteen and having my own kids. So, they didn't call my mother, they called my worker. She came to the courtroom with me and the judge released me to the Department of Family Services caseworker, asking that upon my release I'd be taken out of the state never to return to New Jersey again or she would sentence me to five years at Valentine's Correctional facility for adolescents. All I could think of was how was I supposed to do that when my sons were in New Jersey? The judge made no sense. Who was she kidding? I was supposed to up and leave my babies and just never return to New Jersey? It was time to make decisions. I was going to be charge free, so I had to leave New Jersey; but I'd be back though. All I could do was think of in the back of my mind that the judge was right, and I agreed; but deep down inside when she took those cuffs off me I knew I was coming back. I didn't know when that would be, but at that moment, I was released.

From the caseworker's office, I was released to my aunt and her family, who I've never met these people a day in my life. They were my mom's siblings on her father's side. They were a mixed family, half white half black, but for the most part it was a different kind of family far from where and what I was used to. Now I'm starting all over again at rock bottom when I was just on top of my life. I had to figure out my next move and figure it out fast if I'm going to stay with people I know nothing about. I didn't have Patrick anymore. After stabbing him up there was a court order put in place. Contacting him would be violating my parole agreement, so all I could do was move on with my life.

I'm just thinking about all the things I lost in the process, but I had to take it as a lesson learned and keep it moving. Not saying I really wanted to, but maybe a change was what I needed. I kept starting over, trial and error, fucking up until I get it right, but I was tired of getting it wrong; and it seemed to never go right.

Chapter Ten

Seattle Washington

So what does Seattle Washington have to offer me? What is hitting out here? Judge Jackson made me leave my hometown, now I'm somewhere I really don't know anybody, not even the so-called family I'm moving in with - my aunt Dessie. She was stunning with light red eyes and a redbone. Nice tits, beautiful smile, no ass at all with beautiful curly hair. Dessie and I are the same age, so the other two aunts Coo and Saisa, thought it was a great idea for us to be roommates. It seemed harmless at first, but little did I know she would grow to be envious of me. I was Caramel like Mom, of course I was fluffy cause I have kids, nice buttocks, beautiful titties, and a beautiful smile. She had shoulder-length hair and she was cuter, but my body was better, and my hair was longer. She was still a bomb though. She had one child, a girl, and had a live-in boyfriend. This is where the problem started, so from day one I felt uncomfortable because her man lives with her. I didn't like feeling like the third wheel, or even being around couples. Shit's weird. Real shit, I was homesick, still trying to stay afloat. I knew from the way things were going that the change I was hoping for seemed far off in the distance. It's pretty much the same shit, just different people. Shit, I started questioning why does all my situation end up like this? Maybe I'm the problem and wasn't level-headed enough to understand it.

I missed my children. I felt out of place. Lord knows my next move has to be my best move, so I started thinking. I needed money in the next few days, so I hit the road in full force. I needed a job and my own spot, even though I knew this wasn't a permanent environment for me. That same day I gained employment working at the waffle house making eight-thirty an hour. That's not including tips. I started feeling positive and began feeling a change. I knew it would only take about two months for the money I needed to leave. Yes, that was still the plan, but I still had to live until my departure. The crazy thing is it only took three weeks to save for my apartment. It's just me, so one bedroom is all I needed. That was only five hundred dollars a month, so it was perfect.

I pretty much stayed to myself. After moving in, some fine ass dude name Shawn asked me out, so I kept company with him on my days off; kinda dating and humping. I let him hit and the condom broke, so now we just humped without protection and he didn't know that I was leaving. I wasn't about to tell him anything different. I was grinding and boo macking. Before I knew it I had enough to leave, and I was ready. I actually stayed a few weeks longer than expected, and those few weeks were crazy. I was sick and still trying to work. I thought I had the flu, but I still did it. Now I was on a Greyhound headed home, under the circumstances and scared to fly. Halfway through the ride home, I threw up all over their Greyhound bus. I never throw up unless I am pregnant. My mind was racing. I'm twenty with a possible three kids. I could be overthinking. It could be this week-long ride, but for now I'm almost home, so I put it in the back of my mind.

I got in town and didn't tell anyone. I stayed low, got a room, and began my mission to be a better me. I felt that the very moment I get up, something comes and knocks me down; but I have a plan. First let's see if this includes a third baby. So, before going to the room I run to CVS and grabbed a test to take once I was comfy.

Chapter Eleven

God Has the Last Say

I got a job working at KFC and was painting Apartments to make ends meet. I had to save money so I can get another apartment. I was having a third child Lord knows I wasn't ready for, but I wasn't killing it either, so I need the space for the baby and my sons to come home. I have no time to lose. Moral of the story, I did just that I worked, saved, and moved out the motel. Still, now at twenty years old, my mother wasn't trying to give me my son and she was getting high as hell off crack cocaine, drinking every day and still having her own confusion at home with my stepfather. That just goes to show how men can make you crazy if you allow them to. Read that shit again.

I believe by now she just wanted to keep my son for that check. She was no longer taking care of him as she used to. He was a straight-A student, made honor roll every marking period, and was the teacher's pet. Because he was so respected he was picked for the national spelling bee. She wasn't thinking clearly at all, so she probably was just doing it for the check so she can get high again.

Headed back to my mom house again to have that uncomfortable conversation, of course, she gave me the same spill. No was her answer, and I was pissed. I'm unhappy she just doesn't understand how much being a mother means to me. She makes me feel less than. I'm thinking my boys can keep me out of trouble. Plus I never wanted my boys to feel as if I've abandoned them. I was trying to break the cycle no matter what it took. She felt sorry for all the time she didn't spend with us, so I left him again and took my baby boy Adonis. At least I could be a mother to him until she felt I was well-off enough. Not to mention, she was now getting high. How can you say I'm not a good mother and she hasn't even given me a chance to be a mother? She tries to replace me. I know she loves him, but he is mine and I'm fighting with my mind. I feel like she should have had that same energy raising me and my siblings. How can you fight me for a child I birthed but you never fought for the children you birthed?

With every thought, tears ran down my face as I was no longer able to hide how I truly felt. I felt hushed, stripped of my rights, talked down to - and again, feeling like I wasn't good enough. I feel like when we needed her she wasn't there. Yes I was hurt, but I couldn't let that stop me from loving the son that I have with me already.

Weeks went by with me and my baby boy living my life comfortably. I was fresh off work and settling down to eat my dinner when I hear a loud knock at the door. Now before I tell y'all who it was, I'm just going to say won't he do it. In spite of the circumstances that are happening, I don't have any ill will, but God brought my son to my front door. I'm not talking out of a dark place - I'm talking out of God knowing my heart. He knew I was ready. I wish it were under different circumstances, but it wasn't, and this was the reality.

"Who is it?" I yelled from behind the door.

"The Division of Youth and Family Services of Cumberland County. We need to speak to the lady of the house." they announced.

My first thought was that they're coming for my little son because my mom thinks I'm trying to get my son back. I was never going to cross the only mother I have. I open the door and stood I front of two faces; a white man accompanied by a white female with state badges on. I stepped outside but did not allow them in my apartment to see what they had wanted. They introduced themselves and showed me their identification. They informed me that the cops had found my mother in a hotel and my son home alone due to a call they had received. The blessing was he didn't have an open case. They found my mother in a motel room unresponsive. It seemed she had had an overdose of some sort or she is in a diabetic coma. My mouth dropped wide open, and the first thing came to my mind was where is my child. When I said it out loud they continued to go on with the conversation.

"They have a child in their custody named Quadir who we were told was your son. We would like him to come home at this time."

I cracked the biggest smile, and I said yes, of course. See, the blessing in this was he was never a foster kid. My mother had full custody, so he never experienced what it was to be in the system.

"Good. He's in the car right now. Ca he come in?"

"I don't see why not. I've never had a case with him."

The timing was perfect. I just had this conversation with my mother, and she still didn't want me to have my child; but the way God works, he sent him home any way. He knew it was time for me to be a mother and he sent them to me. I didn't wish any bad towards her. This incident happening to her was just a coincidence. I didn't call her and curse. I prayed. I just let it be and it all worked out for me. It was my given right to be a mother and as tears of happiness fell from my eyes, it felt great.

Chapter Twelve

Motherhood Choices

See what I didn't mention was before that situation with mom, I recently got in touch with my older sister and we started to stay in contact. The day of me and mom's conversation I called my sister Chelle right after. I was hurting, needed an ear, and she is the oldest. I explained how Mom was making me feel, and just express my feelings. Chelle and I became really close after Mom's release from prison. I was venting and crying about how it wasn't fair my mom was trying to replace me, especially because my mom wasn't there for us like she should have been. I was livid, and so was my sister. So Chelle goes and calls DYFS on my mom, knowing she was getting high again. So after DYFS left, I made it my business to call her, because in the pit of stomach I just felt like sis had something to do with it.

I called Chelle and she told me what happened, and how she'd found my mother in the room unresponsive. Chelle used that as the perfect opportunity to help me get my son back home. I was shocked. I did tell Chelle that how she went about it was not okay and I didn't want to go about it like that, even though I knew she was only trying to help me. I had a different plan, but fuck it, what's done is done There's nothing I can do but take care of mine, but now I'm feeling saddened at the thought of what's happening with mom. However, I'm excited because now I have both my sons.

I put them both in the car and we headed to the hospital to check on my mother's condition. I arrived and they sent me directly to ICU. I was confused. I didn't think she was that bad off. This was serious. She had overdosed on top of slipping into a coma. By now my heart is pounding. I'm at a loss for words, but I had to stay strong for my sons although I was terrified; and me being pregnant had my emotions on go. Plus my mind was filled with other things outside of this current situation. I just had a little spat with her, and it got me feeling all bad; but why do I feel like the blame? Because I've grown a mindset that had me feeling like I needed to compete for everything in my life, and afraid to make people upset. Everything I've been through has helped me mask reality, and kind of felt like walking on eggshells. I was afraid of being judged. I was tired of being labeled the aggressor, so yes it does impact my thoughts and emotions on top of my reaction to things.

At this point, my only option is to continue to try to better myself while we happen to go through all this pain. I became really emotionally unstable, mentally unavailable. I had completely tapped out of the actual real world, and it's because I didn't have the proper upbringing. It's also because of my own decisions. Now days the decision to choose right from wrong could be the possibility of why a lot of things did go wrong for me. What I can say is I think more parents should pay attention and listen. I believe that was detrimental in my growing up, and why I'm the way I am today. I won't say that I am insecure, but I have insecurities due to the way life was thrown at me. Pick and choose wisely who you keep your kids around if they mean the world to you. You see from my past that it was family members or friends of the family that put me in harm's way. Be mindful of that and don't ever take things for granted as if it can't happen to you with your kids; because nobody heard me unless it hit close to their home or it was one of their children being tortured. Then they could understand and show compassion.

The moral of what I'm trying to explain is I don't need the feeling sorry for me. How you give back to me is by paying attention. Listen to these babies. Take more time out to pay attention and ask questions. Yeah we may not have the answer to some things, but certain instances can be prevented. Everyone was too wrapped up in their own worlds to even understand everything that I was going through. Nobody even cared, or took a moment to act, but I didn't let that stop that from pushing myself to go even harder to become the person I wanted to become. I knew I had a lot of work to do, but I didn't let it stop me. I would just continue to jump over every hill. I would dig my way out of every hole to make it to the finish line where all of my goals would be met.

What I'm trying to teach in this book is several things. I want the mothers of these young women to understand they must choose between right, wrong, and indifferent. Hear your children out. Their voice matters. Their opinions count. I'll never wait till it's too late to redirect the situation and seek help when you feel there is no way out. I pretty much don't want people to make the same mistakes I have made in my life or repeat the acts that have been done to me against me - nor the mistakes I've made with the people in my life. My main thing was I was not being heard. I was a troubled teen filled with anger, so that's what showed. Not the lovable side, because I really couldn't tell you what the lovable side look liked like. I wasn't really familiar with that. Never make your children feel that way. As far as your parents go, they had a life before us, and we don't know what they had to endure at the hands of their parents or others. I only knew one cycle, and where I'm at now, that cycle is definitely broken.

I've raised my children so they would never have to face the things I've have to. I had no guidance, no nothing. I learned from the bottom up and had to understand that my mother was in the street. Once she became an addict, she was no longer my mother, she was an addict, and a drug she was into came with stealing from your family, abandoned your family, or overdosing. There's a whole lot of sick people and behaviors that come with being an addict, no matter what the drug of choice is. You've definitely got to be stronger to overcome, which is why I took so long to understand my mother's worth. Seeing her for who she truly was, I respect her struggle. With everything she dealt with as a younger child, being a part of the foster care system as well as growing up around family members that were addicts, I think she turned out pretty well. I'm inspired to write my story and inspired by everything because I believe that I owe my mother at least this much. You know my, Tupac Shakur. She is appreciated, because without her I wouldn't be. I inherited her passion. My mother also loved writing and won an award for poetry. All these things I learned about her when it was supposed to hurt them. Let's not make that same mistake. Let's break cycles and try to understand where we went wrong, not point fingers. We're living amongst generations out there that don't have a clue as to how to proceed in a life. There is no clear direction.

I resented myself so much for not really opening up and giving my mom a chance to let me know who she was as an individual. Not the addict, not the daughter, not the cousin or the street runner. I need to know who she was in general. I would have loved her. I think my mother's extra dope, and that's something that wouldn't change for the world.

Chapter Thirteen

When Tables Turn

I get to mom's room, and of course, none of my siblings are here. She has six children, but I was the only child of hers up there, until I heard this loud drained outcry coming from down the hall. My extra ass sister Falisha. She's a year older than me but a year younger than Chelle. My mom's favorite golden child. She always wants to be the center of attention. *'Always trying to be something of importance ass bitch.'* was what I wanted to say, but I could never actually say it. Lord knows I wanted to.

"I've been here at ICU for two hours and you're just showing up doing all this. For what?" I guess she needed a grand entrance.

We meet, greet each other, and I take her to where mom is resting. She was still yelling and crying. The doctors done came and told this fool to calm down, then gave her something to drink. Falisha gets on my damn nerves. After about a minute everything is calm. I go and take a sit next to mommy. I really didn't know what to say, but Ester had kept me in church, and I was no fool to what I needed to do. I slid closer and started praying for her in her ear. I told her I needed her to get up out this coma. I would never be able to explain to my children where their grandma went. They loved her dearly.

"All I can say is, Lord if you hear me, I know my mom is strong. Give her more strength to get through this Lord. I've been through enough pain. I'm not prepared for this Lord. Please give me more time to be more mentally and physically prepared." I prayed as tears began falling like a smooth stream. "How will I cope? I promised to be there for her every step of the way Lord. Please wake her up."

After saying amen, I walked to the waiting area to check on my sons and grab a bite to eat from the hospital kitchen. Of course the boys wanted snacks from the vending machine, and that's just what they got. On my way back I see nurses running towards my mother's room, so I take off running towards the crowd. I get to the room and my mother's eyes are opened. She's looking directly at me out of all the people in the room. All she could hear was me talking to her and praying, so mommy got up. All I could do was cry my eyes out. I broke down both happy and sad. I'm a firm believer prayer works, and she was evidence. She was a living testimony.

I ran to get the boys because she wanted to see them, and I'm sure they missed her. They hugged each other so tight. Maybe an hour or two later mommy and Chelle started arguing. Mom knew that Chelle had called DYFS and the ambulance. I'm just glad mom knew it wasn't me. That's why my son was brought home to me. I'm not that messy, I just moved so different. However, the moral of the story is…won't he do it.

The Lord changes lives and saves them. Mom was due to be released in a week. Come to find out she was back to talking but she lost her mobility. Basically she has to learn how to walk all over again due to having Gout - something that is associated with diabetes. While away at rehabilitation she was getting better. They gave mom a wheelchair and a walker. This was something I wasn't used to, nor was she, but she had to maintain. She wasn't ready for someone controlling her every move and I was around 6 months. Having mom at my house would help me in so many ways. I wasn't buying her no drugs, so that shit was out. She asked instead of going to her house if could she just come live with me and my kids. I told her I didn't mind, but we would have to talk before I made any decisions. I explained that I didn't do drugs and would not allow any around my children. If she really wanted to change, I was there to help, and mom agreed.

I took her to my place, where she expressed how she was tired of that lifestyle and she wanted to take different course. I would help, but sad shit is none of my siblings were around. She has more than just me, but I'll still do my part.

Over the month that passed, me and moms become so close. She was my everything. She taught me some things and I learned so much about the women she is. We were more like best friends, and we shared everything from stories and lots of laughs, to some tears. I was due to have my daughter, so the plan was for mom to be with the boys while I went to have my daughter.

Chapter Fourteen

A New Level of Understanding

I learned my mother wasn't the addict everyone seen her to be. She was strong. She was a queen who had been through more than me as a child, and she admitted she didn't have a clue as to how to mother us. She took her children somewhere she thought would be safe for us, but she didn't know that we would go through so much. She didn't know we would be mistreated. For the first time in my life my mother held me and cried as she kept apologizing. All I could say was I would have chosen been with my addict mother over being in those other living arrangements. I wasn't crying to make her feel bad, I was crying because I was getting clarity. I felt nobody could love me like my birth mother. When I told her about being beat with a baseball bat for not sharing my snack with a cousin, mom was pissed, and she wanted to fight. I saw where I'd gotten my attitude - from my mom. She was ready for war and was behind upset. We continued to talk about the good, bad, and ugly; but it felt great to have her attention without all the extra siblings. That night I could never forget. We laughed all night until we fell asleep. It was the best night of my life.

The next few months were astounding. We learned, she grew, I grew. Yes she was an ex addict, but she belonged to me. She was sober and just living life. I loved who my mother was, sober or not. I'd seen who she truly was, and just like most African American households, we go through so much. Ain't no future in frontin'. She is funny, intelligent - just a jack of all trades. With mom around everything felt different. Years of sobriety went by and Mommy never missed another holiday with me and my kids. She taught me things I couldn't teach myself. In between all things we joined a local church and kept God first, no matter how bad I felt. Life with my mom made it feel different. Mom really got involved. She was the chorus director. Life was great, but the devil knows to attack and when things seem to go well. Mom had a doctor's appointment the following week where she was then diagnosed with heart failure and kidney damage at forty-six years old. She was falling ill so fast and it was just so overwhelming to her. She would sit alone and cry. Even with all this, she was doing her best to change her ways. She was rumbling on, asking why and how but, clearly it's too far gone for that now. She needs to get with some doctors. Her health was in poor standards.

Watching her go through this pain put a lump in my throat. We were right back to where we started, my mind was on overload. Why was this happening now, at a time in my life when I'm trying to figure things out and my mother plays a big part of my process? This was hurting my everyday routine, but I told mom I would be there. We still attend church, and we still would spend so much time together. I was thinking all types of craziness, and I had decisions to make. What if somethings happen and mom passes away? Who would I have then to lean on? Already 20 years old, something had to change. I needed to do something more productive, like going back to school. I needed my GED or something, so I sat to myself and wrote down a few goals. On my list was getting my GED, going to college, a better job, different car, and a bigger house. It was time to put this into motion. So the next day I made a few calls to see where I can start. At 20 years old I needed to know what to do to sign up and attend. I gathered all I needed - and started the Vineland Adult Education Center the next day. For the next eight weeks I was going for my diploma.

The day of testing I sat and prayed to myself, then I went. Once I got to the building I was worried, not knowing what was going to happen. I took it and passed. I cried and hugged my teacher. I felt I'd gotten over one great one hump and I was so excited. Now on to college was all I could think. I was still taking care of mom and taking care of myself, but things were looking up. I know it won't be easy, but I have to do it. I was running myself crazy. Between school, Mom, and my children, I stayed busy. I still had to feed my children, so I need a better career. I also need a better job. McDonalds and KFC ain't paying me enough. If not, I could lose everything. Then what, back to the street life? I felt God didn't bring me this far to drop me off right now. Lord knows all I can do is pray.

I headed back home and got dressed for work. When I got to work about five police cars flew past me. I get to the step and just stood there, taking in the atmosphere. I saw a few of my friends chatting, so I walked over to talk to everyone. They all started running, so I started running. Shit, I'm black. I didn't even know why I was running - I just ran. I hit the corner and got jumped by eight cops. I was slapped, kicked, and punched a few times. I was scared and lost at the same time. What did I just walk into? Why am I being attacked? Everything happened so quick.

Beaten and bloody, I was hauled to jail with no real reason as to why. I was then booked and given papers on which I then saw I was being charged with tampering with evidence, resisting arrest, and assault on eight cops. How is this even possible; but I was in jail, and what made it bad was I had no bail. They claim the assault on the cops left me with no bail, and people with that charge usually have to sit a year. I was devastated. I wanted to be home with my children. How could this have happened? Who would take my sons? A whole year without them, all I could think about was I'd lost everything in just seconds. I was so disappointed in myself. This could have been avoided. Remembering the whole incident, one of the cops grabbed me by my braids and threw me to the ground. Playing the whole thing back in my head, I even pissed on myself out of fear. I couldn't breathe. They put a hurting on me. I was innocent and did nothing wrong other than being in the wrong place at the wrong time.

My mom and aunt came to visit me days later. I explained to them what I was charged with and what I was looking at. My mother and aunt said they would make sure my children were fine, so there were no worries on that end. After the visit I just went back to my cell, sat, and let everything sink in. I just put it in my mind that I'm just going to be in jail until they say otherwise. This was going to be a long-drawn-out process.

Once I got through admissions and processing I was sent to a cell, given a state ID number, and ID. I had no understanding what was going to happen with going to any of this, but I was ready. I got assigned a public defender, who I know from the beginning I was innocent I had no idea what was going on. I explained the situation and he informed me that this process will be long. I would have to sit a year since we were taking it to trial. I explained to my public defender the conversation me and my mother had about this being much deeper than just being at the wrong place at the wrong time. That the individuals that I was standing with had stolen the walkie-talkie from one of the State Troopers that were chasing somebody through the neighborhood. I have no idea about a walkie-talkie or anything to do with the walkie talkies, but I was being blamed for it. He took pictures of all my wounds and explained to me that this will be a way we can win. The cops had literally beat me to a pulp, and I had all the scars to prove it. After our visit, I called home to my mother to fill her in on how my visit went with my lawyer. She informed me that my kids were doing fine, but they missed and wanted to talk to me. My boys were both at school, so I would have to call back later in the week, since we didn't have money on the phone like that.

I knew this process was going to be long, and I was devastated. It was doing more harm than it was good, and I could not wait for it to be over. I was ready to be home already. Mom kept reassuring me that everything would be fine, not to worry about my boys, and everything was under control.

"Don't let the time do you, do the time – otherwise, it's gonna be the hardest thing you'll ever do." Mom advised me.

I've never been to jail for anything longer than a couple of weeks, so they have to sit in a cell for 1 year was too much; but either way, I had to do it. All I kept thinking was this is the big leagues – way different than what I'd experienced. I was with real life fiends, killers and more.

Friday I was scheduled for a bail reduction hearing, and the day wasn't coming fast enough. I was hoping to get a bail that day, but when the damn judge called me a menace to society, I knew that was out of the question. I argued that I was in the wrong place at the wrong time and was attacked by state troopers for being someplace I shouldn't have been. I'm not saying what I did was right, you know being around known criminals, but that was no reason for me to be assaulted, then arrested. All they had to do was question me and they would've known I was innocent. Instead of doing that brough me in on all these trumped up charges to cover their asses for beating me. Regardless of my circumstances, I still had to sit for twelve months before I would receive a bail – which I had already began to mentally prepare for. I knew my chances weren't good, especially with a jailhouse lawyer. He's already told me what I was looking forward to, so I was already looking forward to serving the time. So, I figured I might as well get comfortable. I'd pretty much just lost everything in a blink of an eye and had lost hope. I have no one inside, so I had to live for me now.

My next move was just to get comfortable, since I was going to be here for a while, and to get money on my books. I was trying to be as comfortable as possible, that way this process could be so much easier. I knew a few people already there, so I was pretty much cool. I already had noodles and snacks, so I was pretty much prepared. My main focus was my kids, and I can't even began to explain how exhausted I was. I just wanted everything to just be a dream that I could just wake up from, in my bed. Instead I was waking up to trays out - and making calls on a payphone. This is not okay. I never hit no damn cops. They were trying to justify the foul shit that they had done, but God sees all and there will come a time for them to be judged. Until then, they were the law, and nothing would be done.

I got me a piece of paper and made a homemade calendar to track my time, counting my down my days. One month in, my kids smiling faces came to mind. I had no idea what they though or what they were going through, but I know this process would definitely affect them. I know they miss me. How could I do this to them? I was so disappointed. I just didn't understand what God trying to tell me. Why did he put me in this situation where I was blamed for something I truly did not do and make me sit a whole year? I was really onto something. My life was in order and was coming together. I had plans, goals that I was executing - but now I'm back to square one. I want to get past this phase of my life so I can just move on.

Six months in, I'm lying on my bed and I get a call to go to the social worker's office. Something has happened and they had to tell me - but they couldn't tell me around the inmates of fear that I might harm someone or myself, or cause harm to some apparent authority figure. I went to social worker's office and was approached by four officers and two other staff members. I noticed the phone was off the hook and on top of the desk as I was asked to sit down. Now I was really confused. I didn't know what was going on. A female staff member began telling me that my cousin Jerrell had been beaten to death in an apartment complex out in the neighborhood by some Mexicans. He and his brother broke into someone's apartment and the people were actually in the house. When they broke in the brother got away, but my cousin did not. They found him beaten to death in the apartment. He was pronounced dead on arrival. I sat there silent, confused, numb. I didn't even know how to respond to that. I just sat there quiet as tears just ran down my face. She kept asking me was I okay, but I felt like I was having an out-of-body experience. This couldn't be happening. Not now. I have enough on my fuckin plate. How much more can I take? I was losing all my material stuff and losing people dear to me.

I sat in a trance for about 30 minutes before I snapped out of it. The prison social worker kept saying how sorry she was and let me know that she could allow me some time to myself. Twenty minutes and my tears just wouldn't stop flowing. I couldn't gather my thoughts. I was overwhelmed. She asked me to calm down so I can go back to the population – as if it were that easy. I just was told that my cousin was murdered, and she was asking me to calm down to go back to the population so people can be all in my business. How can you put on a front when your emotions are running high after losing someone; but hey, this is the life I choose. The life I had already been living. So I wiped my tears, nodded in agreement, got up and walked out with two officers beside me.

The whole way back it seemed like that walk back to my cell was so long. At that very moment I just wanted to be close to family. These trying times and my family needed me. I needed them. I needed a hug. I needed to talk to someone. Once I got back to the population I started calling home but no answer. I kept calling until someone finally answered. I spoke with Mom and she pretty much said the same thing the captain and social worker said. I didn't I want to hear it all over again. He didn't deserve that, regardless if he'd broken into someone's house or not. Murder should have never been an option. I think that should have just been handled a different way, but I didn't want to discuss that with my social worker so that's why I just nodded in agreement. His death meant nothing to them. They weren't sincere, and they didn't care.

After I got back of the phone, I went back to my bunk with six other women to be alone with my thoughts.

Chapter Fifteen

Prison Begins with Possession

My current setup was overcrowded and not as clean as it should have been. I hated it. I had a life outside of this place. I just started looking at everything, thinking I should detach so it won't feel so bad. I'm still doing my countdown. After two hours on the phone with my mom, I was relaxed. I guess it was time to grieve and play the waiting game. I ain't back to my normal self, and I don't think I will be for a long time; but for right now I just want to be by myself so I can just cry my eyes out. I had so much to think about but right now.

I've got 10 months in and I was just ready to go. I spoke with my public defender, who informed me that it was mandatory for me to sit one year due to the severity of the crime. He said he put the forms in for a speedy trial and was coming the day after tomorrow.

I completed my 365 days. It sucked, but things were looking promising. Those two months went by fast, and before I knew it I was in court waiting for the judge's decision. When he got done explaining everything and going over evidence, he dismissed the whole case against me with an apology and informed me that the county is not holding me on any other charges. Once I got back to the county jail, I was free to go home. I was so excited yet still devastated because I knew I had to go home and start my life over, in general. I had lost everything, so I had to rebuild. I have lost family, and my family needed me. My sons needed me. It was time I reclaim my life. I wanted to cry again because I was so happy, but I just thanked the judge and the public defender then went about my way. When I got back to the county of course everybody was being nosy. They wanted to know what happened. I explained to them that everything was dismissed, and I was rolling up out of there. I told everybody I was innocent, but today is my day. I gave all my things away I had accumulated. My commissary, my grey sweatpants - you know, stuff like that. I left everybody that would have needed it of course. Hopefully, somebody would have done the same for me.

While packing up getting ready to go, I heard them yell my name to roll up. I grabbed all my things, my mattress, and I run to the door. When I get to the front of the jail to emissions, I looked out the window while they were processing my paperwork. When I see my mother and my two sons, I was so happy. I think that was like the second-best day of my life. I wanted to know everything. Even though it's been a year, did I still have my apartment? Did anybody keep it up for me? Where was my car, and was it still running? My mind was racing as I thought of all the questions I needed answers to. I found out that my dad had gotten my car towed and junked it for a few dollars, with his alcoholic ass. My apartment was still up and running, but barely. I had no electric, no cable, and it looked like people had gone in my house and stole all of my clothes. Because there was no electric and my deep freezer wasn't running, the meat had gone bad and there were maggots falling out of my freezer.

I had just put the key in my door and just took a breath of fresh air. I knew I could start from scratch and planned on doing that after evaluating my home. Then I just sat. I talked with my mother for a few moments, and she didn't look like herself. Of course, she knows her health was still taking a toll on her, but I said nothing to her. I thanked her for looking after my children and making sure no harm or danger came their way while I was away. I told her that I appreciated her for giving that much energy while she was sick. I didn't expect her to do that, but she did, and she's stuck by me the whole time as a mother should have. I wanted her to know just how much I loved her.

After a conversation we got cozy, popped us a bottle of wine, and got to cleaning my apartment. We threw out so much filth and wiped cobwebs down as I played slow jams. It was moments like this that I missed, being locked up. Once we finished cleaning up I got myself together and started thinking about everything that needed to be paid. It was getting dark, so I had to light candles, but I didn't mind. I stayed there in my apartment with my candles burning, my music playing, and my cup of wine as I come up with a plan. I have my life back, was still young, and still trying to figure life out. I didn't feel like my life was over, I was just getting a late start.

I was still a little pissed because they had stolen all my things. Where was the love? Damn. I'm going to go through more stress knowing I'm backed up in bills, and my dad still ain't said nothing about my car he sold because I left it on his property. He felt he needed to junk it because he needed the money for a bill. I didn't know I had to support these people. I just said fuck it. My bills were backed up, I had no car… what was I going to do?

Here I am a year later and all I had was $20 to my name. All I can think about was hitting the bar and having a few drinks. I saw a couple old friends and we headed back to my apartment after I warned them that I had no lights, but I had candles and was just getting everything back up and running. I still had a little cleaning to do, so my friends helped me clean up before we smoked and sipped a little. Jen, Tasha, and I were reminiscing about the old days. Even though there were no lights, we were basically on some regular hood shit. I'm sure there was about ten other houses in the hood that didn't have electric, so that was a normal thing, which is sad - but true.

While cleaning Tasha brought up this guy who sold weed and other drugs that she didn't like – him or his girlfriend. He had money, so she suggested we rob them. That would erase all my problems was my first thought, but I just came home. What if we get caught? I was sitting around trying to make moves to better my situation right now, but honestly, what else was I supposed to do? Me going back to work would take too long - and doing anything outside of that was just too much. So, being young and ready to do whatever to get back my life that I once knew, I was with the robbery shit.

So, we were supposed to have called a few people and got a ride to these people's house. I was supposed to be the one to knock on the door to tell him that my car had broken down and that I needed a jump, or that I needed to use their phone. That's exactly how it. Went when we got there it was just the one girl by herself, so I asked to use the phone and she allowed us in. I forced her in the bathroom and stripped her of all her jewelry. Of course. she was screaming and crying.

"Shut the fuck up and give me everything!" I barked.

We had a body to go to each room in the house. The living room, dining room, basement, bedrooms, etc. We flipped the whole joint, and we found nothing in the house. No drugs, no money, nothing. So basically we were robbing these people for the practice. By the time I left the only thing I had was a few coins, a couple cell phones, and some jewelry. I could have gotten that off of a street lick on the corner or robbing a junkie. You feel me. So now I'm just mad as hell because of the fact that we could've gotten caught and gone to jail for nothing.

So anyway, we finish the robbery and get up out of there. As we're leaving out of the door Tasha says my fucking name, so I said to her, "I thought we weren't using our government? What is you doing?!" I feel like she tried to set me up, throwing my government out there. So now this lady in the bathroom knows my name, and all I could think was that I was going back to jail as we jump in our car and take off. We go back to the hood and everyone goes their separate ways. I go to my mother's. I'm over here chopping it up with her and I had just let her know what I had done - and that I had fucked up somewhere along the line. My mom started crying.

"Why would you do that?" she asked.

"I feel hopeless. Me getting a job isn't an option. I just lost everything. I feel defeated."

She continued to cry and told me that she would still be there for my kids. I didn't want to put that pressure on her, but honestly, it really kept out her out of trouble. It kept her from getting high and thinking of the street life. Anyway, I gave her what I had and prepared to leave her house. "Call me if anything happens." she said to me as I walked out her door.

I returned to my house still in the same situation as when I left, because I'd robbed someone for nothing. I was kicking myself in the ass because I just said I wasn't getting into any more trouble, but here my young dumb ass was, back in some shit. I was even more pissed about the fact that this bitch said it was drugs and money in the crib, then we get there and there was nothing. Now the cell phone that I stole from the spot just kept on ringing. I'm at my crib and dumping everything from my pockets just in case the cops run down on me I don't have nothing that I stole from this lady's house on me. I need a bottle. I am stressed to the max because I know it's going to go down.

This phone is steady ringing, so I picked it up and disguised my voice. I answer, "Hello." in a male's voice, and a male's voice came through the other end.

"Buddha I know this you, and I know you got my girl's shit.", this this that and the third.

Mind you, I ain't saying shit. I'm just listening and let him say what he was going to say, then I banged on him. I was definitely not having a conversation with a nigga on a stolen ass phone to incriminate myself. I didn't even turn off the iPhone, I stomped it - because they probably could track me by just having that phone. Even if I would have sold the phone it was still coming back to me of course because somebody was going to snitch over the phone. My regular cell started ringing and I see it's Tasha calling. I pick up the phone and she tells me that she was just arrested before she kept asking me where I was at. I told her I was out of town and hung up. I felt like everything was closing in on me, but I wasn't trying to get caught just yet. I just came home, and who want to go back to that cell? Them four walls don't say anything.

I wonder how did they get Tasha and why she's asking where I am? I started sweating and my heart began pounding. I walked in my house and decided to try to eat something, but I couldn't even eat. I just stared at the wall and asked myself, "What did you do? I held my head in my hand and tried to come up with a solution. Either way, I know my boys were staying out of the system. I knew I was going up the river and I was so upset with myself. My mom assured me I was going to be okay and she would make sure everything was all right and she wouldn't leave my side, but I was wrong for doing what I did.

I spent that night in my apartment getting drunk as hell. I smoked about a quarter of some skunk and just laid in the dark with my candles burning. I can't handle just lying there, so I got up. I couldn't just be laid up in the crib because I knew if they had my name then they had my address. I walked out the door and went to get a cigarette from the loosie lady. That's the only thing I didn't have was cigarettes. I needed to clear my mind and just breathe in some fresh air. I had been in the house for a while and didn't want to be there. I know shit was going down, I just didn't know when. So I want to get me some E&J and a few losses, then I went to my homegirl's house.

We rolled up and were in the middle of smoking a Dutch when I hear this shuffling noise outside of the window. I'm still smoking on my Dutch, so I'm like, fuck it. I know it was the police and that they were coming to get me, but at least they were going to take me high. Boom! Boom! Boom! Boom! They state who they are and order us to open the door. They informed us as to who they were looking for and say my name. The lady of the house opens the door as I'm standing against the wall smoking my Dutch. They bypass everybody else, go up to my co-defendant and he puts her in cuffs. They knew exactly who she was, so clearly some told. They never even walked up on me, so I don't think they knew what I look like, but I still was hitting my Dutch. One of the officers looked down at the picture on the paper he had and looked up at me.

He said, "Oh, you're who I'm looking for. Do you know what I'm here for?"

"Yeah. Just let me finish smoking and you can take me." was my reply.

A female officer came over and said, "Put your hands up. Let me check your pockets."

Oh yeah, she let me finish smoking my Dutch. Meanwhile, my homegirl's falling all out, crying. I don't know why the hell she did the crime if she knew she couldn't do the time. I had just done it yesterday, so it wasn't nothing to me. I'm going back to jail, and ain't no telling when I'm coming home. The cop introduced herself, put me in cuffs, read me my rights, and hauled my black ass off to jail.

Here I go, strolling my ass back up into this County jail. Everyone was looking at me, wondering why I was back when I had only been home a couple of weeks. I only got home to have nothing, so I only did what any nigga would do, which was get it to do by any means necessary. So, of course they assigned me my cell, give me my docket number, and I'm back sitting in a cell again with no bail. "Menace to Society" is what the judge called me, and I was sure I was sure proving him right. Of course they didn't give me a bail, and even if they did give me a bail, where was my family getting that bread from? We didn't have it like that and were barely making ends meet. My only option was to just sit and wait for Belva Dakshin. Even if I got a bail reduction wasn't nobody coming to bail me out. You know how I know this? They couldn't even keep my little apartment afloat, which is why I'm even back in this situation. So I guess I'll be here until the judge sees fit.

I know I'm going to prison this time. I don't know how much time I'm going to do, but I know I'm going to be 21 years old and I'm thinking if it ain't life, it ain't long. I ain't going to be here forever, so I basically give up. I would've never thought my people in the hood would be crying wolf. These motherfuckas gave my government and then some, so I got the most time out of everybody. How do I get the ringleader charge when the robbery wasn't even my idea? That didn't even make sense; but because they all told on me, I had to wait to go to trial to even be sentenced. By this time everything was said and done, I had already been in the county for 18 months, and that's how long it took for my case to be finalized. They sentenced me to seven years. The first plea bargain was 25 to life, and I hadn't even killed nobody. My lawyer came back with that offer, which had me crying and screaming. I couldn't do that much time. I'm too you, and kids to get back to who couldn't be without me that long. She went back to talk to the prosecutor and came back to offer me 15 with an 85.

"You didn't do nothing to help me at all. Who are you working for, me or them?" I asked in a raised voice.

She asked me to give me her a second chance to go back into the courtroom to see what more she could do. She came back with another offer.

"They'll agree with 7 years with 85%. You'd do 4 and 1/2 years and 3 on parole." she informed me.

I had no choice but to agree with the offer. I already had almost two years in, so I was okay with that. Not really okay, but again, what other choice did I? I had to do the time regardless. They sent me back to the county after my sentencing date and I was pretty much ready to go to prison. I wanted this whole ordeal to be over with, in spite of me putting myself in that situation. I just wanted it to be done with. I felt like once I got the prison the quicker this would be over.

Prison was a whole 'nother life for me. I knew my life would change, but not like this. I went back to keeping to myself, and I pretty much sat in shock for so long. I was so appalled at a seven-year sentence for a crime where nobody got hurt, killed or anything. Not to mention, it was my first crime as an adult. How do they give me this much time? They clearly were using me as an example. I pretty much was only serving maybe a year-and-a-half or two before I was released. That's not bad, but I still had three years to do on parole. I like to smoke, drink and all of the I wasn't going to be able to do. I messed up and I'm right back in the same situation. I can't and I won't forget the day that I did that.

I knew I really need to grow up. I don't know what God was trying to prevent, but I think that's exactly what it was. I believe he was trying to settle me down. He put me away for a year prior to this to tell me to chill, relax, and stay out of the way; but I came home and did exactly what he tried to prevent, so I only got what I was asking for pretty much. Madison is just a pill I was going to have to swallow. I put myself in the situation, so I was going to do the time and be done with it. That was it. Things could have been worse. I mean I could have been looking at life, but yet I'll get another chance at this life thing. Until then, I'mma just sit and do my time.

It was almost my time be transferred to prison and I still couldn't believe at 21 years old I was on my way to prison. The drive up was beautiful. There were so many mountains. I knew I was close to the prison because there wasn't anything around but trees. It was way different than county, and I understood I was going to be up here with the big dogs - lifers, people who have nothing to lose that were never seeing sunlight again; but I'm here to do my time and not make friends while awaiting my release date, which was July 26th. Of course I got that at sentencing because I have a mandatory sentence, the same as I received the previous year.

When I got to reception they gave me boots, uniforms, and toiletries. They took me to my housing unit, which was Max. I can remember the layout it was the same as the county, and these women were on a different level because these were people here for the rest of their life and pretty much had nothing to lose. I knew I had to be on my A game and stay out the way, so of course I dabbled in Islam and just became one with myself, which kind of calmed me. I was a turned-up teenager, so that made me calm down a lot, and I started hanging out with the Muslims. Not saying I was going to change overnight, but a change was definitely in the making. I was definitely going to make myself known, because I heard different stories about being in jail and I definitely didn't want to be that chick, so I came down there and was quiet. I wasn't really talking to too many people but was being observant, checking out the scenery - seeing who was in charge and who wasn't. You know, learning my space and just trying to make the best out of a bad situation.

My stay in prison definitely wasn't a layup. I definitely had my share of fights, debates, lockups, and other stuff - but that's prison. When I first got there, I shared the bunk with some big raggedy black phat bitch with missing teeth From Newark New Jersey. Most chicks there feared her because of how tall she was, but I wasn't about to be one of them. I wasn't looking for trouble, but I wasn't going to run from no one. I had a reputation to uphold, so I moved according to how everybody else moved and just stayed out the way. This one day though she wanted to try her luck with me. We shared the same cube and she felt like she wanted to bully me, just saying a bunch of nonsense; but what she didn't know was I was a whole savage on ice. She was talking crazy, so I let her know I'm no punk and bitches jump up just to get beat the fuck down. I was in rare form. This bitch had everyone else spooked, but not me. I fight. She thought because I was little she was just going to son me, so I went back and forth for about 2 minutes too damn long. I walked off the wing to go smoke a cigarette, figuring when I came back in I would be a lot more calm - trying to diffuse the situation; but nope, this monkey was still at it. I nicely shut the door to the wing, walked up on her and swung. I hit this big bitch bout six times before she knew she'd even been struck. I jumped back and gave her a chance to fight me. You could tell by the look in her face she had never been hit with such Force and so many times by such a small person. By then I had made it known that I wasn't to be fucked with.

I guess the rest of my bid was a little easier. I had a couple more scuffles, but I did the bid fairly easily. I engaged in the whole lesbian thing and had a couple girlfriends. I just tried to make my jail time as easy as possible. I knew I had to be there for a while, so I did what I had to just to survive. I had to prove a point to her since she felt like because she was big whatever that I was just going to be a punk, and that's what I wasn't. Life had thrown so much shit at me, so what the fuck could she do to me that life hadn't already? Still, my best bet was to challenge her and get my respect. The moral of the story was she pretty much was beaten bloody. Different inmates came down right away to help me clean up the blood. This genius runs off the wing screaming she got jumped by several female inmates, which was a lie was. She just got that ass whooped, so now we should be cool and there should be no misunderstandings.

While she's running off down the wing screaming, I went back to my bunk and sat down like nothing happened, waiting for the Doom Squad. The Doom Squad are these officers about thirty deep with the shields, big ass stick, and cans of Mace - so when you see them, you run. I knew they were coming, so I went inside. Everybody knew that they would fuck you up, and they wouldn't be beating my ass that day. I was just lying there when they came down the way. Everyone was cool, playing cards and watching TV; but nobody was out of place, so who could they attack? The come onto the wind and asked me did I hit the girl and I denied everything. He checked both of my hands for blood or bruises, which I had none, so they sent me on my way and took her to the crisis because me and everybody on the wing said she did it to herself. Crisis then moved her off the wing completely, so I got that bottom bunk anyway that she fought so desperately for. I stole all her commissary – cosmetics, Walkman… anything you could possibly think of. I just scraped your name off of it. She had pretty much nothing, so I was set. Maybe next time she will know to pick on somebody else, so she learned a lesson. They cleared count and everyone was moving around like nothing happened. It was back to a regular prison day I guess.

During my time I signed up for Life Skills, Parenting, Anger Management, and GED classed. I took all types of classes and I learned all these certificates. I proud of myself and knew there were all things I would need out in the real world. I even got into a craft shop where I would make things for my sons. I would read a book to them on a tape then send the book and the tape back home so they can hear me read it to them. I made them clothes, slippers, cards, and pictures. They were still kind of young, but they wrote back. It was the highlight of this dark time. Maybe three weeks before I was set to be released I got a letter in the mail from home. I didn't think nothing of it because my Mom wrote me. When I opened it, inside was a newspaper clipping detailing how my little brother had been murdered in his home. He was shot three times and died on the spot. D.O.A. He was left in the streets to die like a dog. I dropped the letter instantly and my body when into shock. I felt dead. It felt like my soul left my body and my spirit collapsed. A part of me just died. My little baby brother was gone. Why did I have to come to this jail? I could have saved him, or at least I hoped. We could have fought together for our lives, but I was stuck in here when he needed me the most. I had so many thoughts running through my mind. I was in a state of shock and all could do was cry myself to sleep.

I think the next thirty days went by and I didn't speak to or interact with anyone. I was lost, and I had questions I needed answered. Why did it happen? Who was he with? What did he look like when my mom went to ID his body? I remember them saying he was shot in his face. Mom said he had a hole in his eye duct and his was swollen and shattered due to the bullet. He also had defensive wounds, which showed he was fighting for his life. At least I know he tried; but there was more than one suspect, so I'm proud. He lived in an upstairs apartment, so he had to travel down maybe 16 steps to make it to the street. He did, and he made it down the street before collapsing lifeless. It was investigated, but we got no results. We all know how the street works, you don't talk. Snitches get snitches and thrown in ditches; but of course, those fuckers ain't doing nothing. It basically felt like nothing was really investigated because it was just another black man and they'd be wasting taxpayer dollars. So you know they really didn't care. They went back to doing their same everyday shit while we were left to pick up the pieces. Mom told me after about three or four weeks they labeled it a cold case after three or four weeks. Can you believe that? I feel like four weeks is not a long enough investigation, so when I come home I'll have to hire my own detective. Something has to give. That would just be my way of giving back to him because I felt like I couldn't be there to save him. I wasn't there to save his life, and that would haunt me forever. This has been the worst pain I've had to endure, besides everything else in my life. I need to finish my bid and get back to my family. My days are numbered, and I had so much to do. I could smell freedom. I could feel it. There were so many people I needed to see and so many things to do; and on July 26th, I was able to begin so.

On July 26th at 10 am I was asked to roll up - the same process as a county. I walked towards the Ivory City exit gate like I hit the lottery. The ride back to South Jersey took a few hours, so I didn't make it home until about 3:30 that afternoon. All I could think of was seeing my kids. I knew they'd gotten so big. Besides seeing them, I need a bath and a change of clothes and a drink. I really wanted to smoke a Dutch, but my parole officer wasn't trying to hear that. Since I couldn't smoke a Dutch, I had to keep it cool, get us a drink and stay drug-free.

When I finally made it to my mom's house to see my sons, the look in their eyes when they saw me cannot be explained. I was nothing but pure love. They ran and jumped in my arms. They hugged me so tight and asked me to never leave us again. All I could do was hug them tighter as I vowed to never go back to prison - and I meant just that. I knew what needed to be done, so I was going to do what I had to, to keep focus. My children depending on me to succeed. After my moment with them, I wanted to hug my mother. She was crying and laughing at the same time. She was so excited. She looked weak, but strong. I could tell she wasn't getting any better and her health was taking a toll on her; but she was still alive and kicking, so that's all that matters. I've been losing folks left and right, so I don't think I would survive if I lost her. We hugged for what seemed like forever, talked about my experience, and what she had been through without me as well as what my children had to face. How they felt, and what my goals were. I got paroled over to my mother's so I can be with my sons and help assist her with her day to day issue, so I was okay; but I couldn't be there long, I have things to do. I need to get my own place, a job, a car, and back into the college. I needed to really focus on me and what I needed my life to look like.

Bright and early Monday morning I made a few calls to the school where I received my GED, picked it up and went to the college to register. After leaving there I hit the temp agency with my prison ID, and of course that ain't look good; but that day the lady actually gave me a job and sent me to a factory the next morning. I'd crossed two of my goals crossed off the list - three more to go. I'll be catching a bus everywhere until I save up for a car, and living with my mom was good for now, since she could really use the help. I could really use the help as well while I'm getting my life in order. I stayed busy to stay out of trouble and out the way. I reported every week until I got a regular schedule, then I would only have to report once every two weeks, which makes you feel less like you're still in prison.

Over the next few weeks I worked and went to college where I majored in Rehabilitation Counseling - because my whole life I have been wrapped up in drugs and street life, so I thought I'd help people of that classifications. I feel like if can I help my mother get off drugs, I can help people shake anything. A drug addict is no different from being a gambler, prostitute, or pastor. These are people too, and if I can help, that's what I'd like to do - but I knew it wasn't going to be easy.

Everything was going nicely. I opened a bank account and started saving money for the place and car I needed. I'd been through so much, I used it as my motivation, my strength. I stayed prayed up and read my Bible regularly. I felt like this was my last chance to get it right and make my mama proud, so I continued working and going to school. My next goal was to be driving, so I went to DMV and got my permit. I needed a car, and I needed it now - the legal way. I wasn't doing anything illegal. Everything was straight by the book. Squares as a pool table. It was boring, but hey, beats being in jail.

About a year-and-a-half after my release, my mother's kidneys have failed. It was always something. She was put on dialysis and heavy medication daily just to keep her from feeling the pain. The shunts they had put in she kept rejecting, and she told me she couldn't take the pain. I could tell she was trying to maintain for and the kids, and I needed her. It didn't matter how much pain she complained of being, I still wanted her to be around. We didn't know how we were going to explain this to them, so she dealt with it uncomfortably. They had to take the second shunt out of her and try it again, but she wasn't a young girl anymore. She was old G, and her illness was kicking her butt. I just wanted to help her make her as comfortable as possible, but there was nothing I really could do. She told me that the dialysis was really painful, makes her cramp really bad, gives her cottonmouth and causes her back pain. She was experiencing so much discomfort, and all I wanted to do was make her as comfortable as I could at this time, so I went back and forth between the doctor's, school, and work. I was mentally drained; and let's not forget parole had a hook in my back to make sure I was doing everything I needed to do. I was still feeling drained after reporting, so I called up a friend. I needed a girl's day out like – hair, nails, etc. Then I planned to hit the casino, just to get my you know mind off all the things I've been dealing with, and to see if I can hit big. Who knows? I hit up my homegirl Tee, who I hadn't spoken to in years, but it was worth the shot. She was excited and agreed to come with me to the casino. Atlantic City here we come! I knew Mom was sick, but Lord knows l needed that break.

I went back to the house, did my hair, put my babies to bed, then hopped my big ass on the bus to meet with Tee at Bally's Casino. I wore an all-black wrap-around dress, and knee-length boots with a royal blue and blue clutch bag. My sew-in was cut into a Bob, I wore hazel contacts, and silver accessories to match.

Your girl was definitely big sexy at her finest. Shit, I was feeling myself. I was at an all-time high and it'd been a while since I felt like this. I got off the bus after the long transit ride to Bally's, and about ten minutes after I arrived I spot my girl across the room and waive. My homegirl is about 5 feet with a chocolate complexion, and hair down her back. She's Jamaican and Spanish, which is one hell of a combination. Big 'ol titties and a flat ass. You know, a regular chubby chick, but you couldn't tell her stuck-up ass shit. This bitch thinks she is above and beyond people. She's bougie beyond bougie and always carried this 'I'm better than you' attitude; but she was straight from the hood, so don't ask me why she thought she was a damn celebrity. Bitch was regular like you and, except she can do some hair. She worked full-time at a salon in Newark. Her mom lived in my town, so she was always around. Yes she pissed me off a lot, but that was one of my friends; and she don't like everybody just digging in my head.

Anyway, I walked up to her to see she is wearing a tight fitting, one-piece zebra jumper that showed off crazy cleavage, bright red pumps, red hair, and a pound of makeup. She was cute, but her attitude made her ugly as fuck; but she was still my friend, so I had to make the bitch feel like she was cute. Who was I to judge anyway? We exchange hugs and kisses before we started vibing to a Jay-Z track while sitting at the bar drinking. Yep, my stupid ass was drinking, which was something I cold pee right out, as opposed to smoking. It was girls' night out, and I was ready to get the party started, so we ordered two Long Island Iced Teas and two double shots of Hennessy – hold the ice. That Hennessy was so nasty, but the music was on. They were playing hit after hit and I could feel the bass throughout my body, as I slowly moved to the music, catching every beat. I look around for Tee and spot her dancing with some big white baldheaded motherfucker with blue eyes who's watch cost a nice piece of change. See, back in the day my girl Tee was a call girl. She's getting real sexual with this dude, so I'm hoping she's not about to fuck this white boy.

We partied and drank for the next eight hours. By then, her and this white guy were on their way to the elevator. She's waiting for me halfway across the room, waving to get my attention.

"What's up girl?" I asked when I approached her at the elevator.

"I'm gonna go upstairs to his room. He told me he got a suite on the 15th floor."

Clearly those suites were for celebrities only, so he definitely had to be somebody. So I said, "Okay, I'll go with you - just to be safe. I don't want you getting yourself into no drama or whatever."

The whole ride on the elevator, this man has gun on display, and lets us know he didn't allow people in his room. I guess he was pretty much giving us a warning so if we get any ideas about trying to rob him or anything like that that he would shoot us. At least that's what I got from it. So we got up to the suite, and it was beautiful. Big, tall windows, a big ass jacuzzi, and it had a winery. There was one floor that had anything you could possibly think of, and flat screen TV's everywhere. I felt like a queen at that moment and I was dreaming. As soon as we got off the elevator, I took off my heels before me and Tee started looking around. I was extremely tired after dancing for 8 and consuming about 15 drinks along with 5 shots. Now Tee has my ass up in this man's room.

I doze off, tired as hell from the night, and I wake up to yelling and screaming. Tee is yelling at this man, "No, I'm not fuckin' you!"

"You played me! You had me bring you up here, thinking we were fuckin' and now you're telling me you're not?!"

This man is pissed off ad looked like he's ready to pull out and shoot our black asses. I was just ripped from my sleep, so I'm trying to get my balance, then get to my girl who's still going back and forth with this dude.

"Let's just go. We need to get up outta his room now!" I spat at Tee.

I see dude out of the corner of my eye rummaging through a cabinet of some sort and bring it to Tee's attention. She tells him she's just going to leave, but he's still pissed. Trying to diffuse the situation, I ask, "What's going on here?"

"This fucking bitch told me she was going to fuck! I brought her up here, spent all my money on her, and she didn't! She played me!" he yelled before going on a rant, threatening to throw her out of the 15th floor window and that remind us he has a gun. "Don't ever play with me! Y'all better Google Hammy's!"

He went on rambling about things that didn't even concern us, so I'm starting to get scared; but I also knew if things got too crazy we could always jump his ass. I get Tee's attention so we can slide out, but she's still going back and forth with dude as she tries to get past him. He grabs her and begins yelling as she tries to fight him off. She finally gets away from him and runs across the room to me. I grabbed her arm and we take off running for the elevator. I pushing the call button about fifteen times, begging the elevator door to finally open so we can get on the elevator and away from this man before he pulls out this gun he's been talking about all night and kill us. I really don't know what's going on, and I don't even care. I just want to get off the 15th floor. The elevator door pops open, we jump in and we hit the button for the lobby. He was so close behind us that I can hear his footsteps as he's yelling, trying to catch us before the elevator closed.

We get down to the lobby and bust out laughing. I mean, laughing so hard we fell to the floor.

"Never again!" I scolded her jokingly. "Bitch, you always got me in some shit!"

"I don't be trying to though; but it was a good night, even though we almost got killed."

We headed to get on the bus, since she knew I had to be at parole the next morning. Oh, I didn't mention I ended up smoking a Dutch when I got into the men's room. What was I thinking? Never again. I couldn't wait to get home. I kissed my friend before we parted ways, and we promise to keep in touch. I get to the bus stop, I'm waiting on the bus, and I couldn't help but to think, *'What the hell did I get into?'*. Although, it was one hell of a night. I had to work later on that night, and I had some homework I had to do, so it was back to the drawing board.

I needed a bath and some comfortable clothes badly. Twenty minutes away from the house, I called my mom and told her to unlock the door since I would be in shortly. I knew I had to get back to handling my business.

One week later, I was scheduled to take my driver's test, which I of course passed, so I am now a legal driver. Now all I have to do is finish saving up for my car, which I wasn't too far off at all. I already had about $2,300 saved up, and the car I wanted was $3,000, so I just needed about $700 more -which was about two more checks. It was a cream Lexus with tan interior, chrome rims, a sunroof, and it drove real sweet. I test drove it like two weeks prior, and it was so me. The next few weeks flew by, and I was getting it. I felt like I finally really getting somewhere, and I was really feeling accomplished. When I did get my car I had no payments, but I had to pay for insurance, which I probably wouldn't have to pay a lot. What mattered most was I was now able to cross the car off my list of things to do. Next was to put a plan together to get me an apartment or a house in a better area for my family. I'm family-oriented, so it had to be somewhere I could raise a family while in college, working and complying with parole - as far as they knew.

My mom was okay, so I was able to focus on the rest of my to do list. A house or an apartment was cool, but I was getting older and a house would suit me and my son's best. So I beat the block, moving every rock and board until April when I saw a For Sale sign on one of the properties. It belonged to a Russian couple. I decided to take a chance and pulled my Lexus up into their driveway. I approached, introduced myself, and asked to speak to the woman of the house. I let her know I was in need of housing and filled her on a little on my situation. I also let her know that I was on a housing program and she would be receiving guaranteed money every month. By the end of the conversation she'd told me she'd be willing to rent to me until she was able to sell her home, but she'd need to talk it over with her husband and would get back to me. So, I left her my number, hopped back in my car, and crossed my fingers – hoping to hear back from her. Two days later she actually gave me a call. She told me to come up with $2,400 and I could move in. I couldn't think of any words that could describe how I was feeling. I was really making things happen. I now had a house now, attending college and working. I had a bank account, my mother's health was going great, and my kids were good. Life was at an all-time high. Now all I needed to do was get this money up for the deposit for the house, which I fell in love with. The inside was beautiful, and immaculate. When you walked in the front door the first thing you saw were the glass sliding doors, which were mirrored, so you saw yourself when you walked inti the house. There were seven different sections of this house, one of which held three bedrooms and a sunroom. The other side of the house had two more bedrooms, two bathrooms, a garage, three sheds in the back and sliding doors. There was even a vacuum cleaner that would adjust to the actual wall socket. The doors didn't open and close regularly, they slid out of the walls. It had a big ass front yard surrounded by a white, picket fence, and it even had a pond. I had to have this house; and who says that black people can't get no big ass house with a white picket fence? At the age of twenty something years old I had mine, and we were only the second black family in this neighborhood, so you couldn't tell me I wasn't a queen. I knew my kids were going to love it there. They had all the space they needed to ride their bikes and not worry about being shot, kidnapped or none of that. We could just enjoy.

I was going to work extra hard to get this money up. I told the landlady to give me three weeks, and I would be in touch. I knew the clock was ticking and I had money that needed to be made. Did I mention it there were only two black families in the neighborhood? If I did, I'm going to mention it again; and to top it off it was right around the corner from my school, so that was that was dope.

For the next four weeks I worked doubles, triples, and I went to school. I needed this house. I called the lady as soon as I got the money, we met up, and I hugged her so tight. I have a nice house, I'm driving a Lexus, working, and in college. You can't tell me nothing; and with Christmas right around the corner, all I could think about was the beautiful Christmas my kids would have. I missed a lot of time from their lives, so I planned on making it up to them starting with Christmas. So I could make this Christmas happen for my kids, I took out a $5,000 loan. They'd missed out on so much, and I just wanted to make my mom and kids proud – and show the world that even after all I'd been through, I was still able to come out on top. I was a shining star, and nothing could stop that; at least that's what I thought until I got a 911 call at work informing me that my mother had been taken to ICU. Her sugar had shot up to 213, which was high enough to send her into a diabetic coma. I dropped to my knees in horror. I just couldn't believe after all the good that was happening the devil still had a different plan. He still wanted to steal my joy. Why was this happening now? I wanted her to come to the new house and stay over some nights, but she had to get through this first.

I leave work and rushed to the hospital. I think I did about 120 in a 60 mph zone the whole way, until I brought my car to a screeching halt outside the hospital. I signed in and made my way to the elevators, hyperventilating until the elevator stopped on her floor. I got off on the fourth floor and see my grandmother and her husband sitting in the waiting area. I stopped to say hello and gave her a hug. She began to repeat to me the information she had been given regarding her condition. She told me that it was bad this time, and that they were hoping and praying she made it out of this one. This was the second comma in three months. She was really putting up a good fight, and I knew just how strong she was, but this was going to be her hardest fight of all. I was told to talk to her, like I did last time. I just hoped I would get the same results.

I walked into her room and paused. She had all these tubes and wires coming from a body and her nose. She was really in bad shape, and I didn't know what I could do to help. I pulled a chair up to her bedside, grabbed my Bible, and I started to read a scripture. I went back to what I knew, which was being a Christian. I knew without a doubt after surviving everything I've been through that prayer works, and God was able. I knew besides the streets that did all this to her that God would have the last say. So I read, prayed, and of course I talked to her about everything and anything. Even though she couldn't respond, I was still talking, just hoping she can still hear me and my prayers. I repeated the same routine for the next four days. I started to give up when her heart machine started flashing and making noise. She had just started breathing on her own. The doctors and nurses rushed into the room, so I moved out of the way so they could do their jobs. Her eyes were open, but she wasn't talking and didn't have that much strength; but her eyes were open, so I knew she was woke and that was a start. I seemed that ever since my mom stopped getting high and living a normal like if what took a toll on her body because her it was so immune to the drug – and once she stopped it made her sick. I felt that her not getting high made her die faster. Not only did the dialysis make her sicker, it was killing her faster. From the age of 17 years old up until now her body was clearly immune to the drugs and she could do all the regular stuff everybody else could - but the minute she started living right her body gave up, slowly killing her. I guess my mother's life was a your damned if you do, damned if you don't type of situation; but whatever she had to do to get better, I was gonna be there to help every step of the way. For now, we needed to work on her talking and walking again. She couldn't go back home and had to go to a rehab center to become strong enough to live alone, so I had to be the one to tell her the news.

When I broke the news, of course she cried and mumbled, "I'm tired."; her first words after the four-day coma she was in. She went on to say she was tired, then she signaled with her hand for me to give her a pen. I found a small pencil and notepad then handed it to her. She wrote, "Thank you for always being by my side, even when I wasn't by yours at times. I heard everything you said while I was asleep, and Mommy is so sorry." She went on to say how she was in pain and getting tired of fighting. She also said she would rather die than to feel how she does. I immediately began crying.

"Stop talking like that. You have to fight, just like you taught me to. Be a fighter. I had to fight, now it's your turn."

She began to write on the notepad again then handed it to me. She wrote, "I can't walk, can barely speak… what man is it going to want a woman can't speak and can barely take care of herself. I would be a burden to a man."

"You shouldn't be worried about a man right now. Just focus on getting better Mom."

After I further explained her new living arrangements, Mom was on board. I helped move her in, got her a couple of nightgowns, slippers, panties, and bras. I wanted her to want for nothing while she was there getting better. I was also checking in everyday after work or school and bringing up things she needed. Thanksgiving was coming in a few weeks and Christmas was right after. I wanted her strong so she could be home for the holidays and enjoy family time. I just wanted to spend any moment I could with her. Tomorrow isn't promised, and there was no telling how much longer mom would be here. While she was here, I was going to enjoy my baby.

All this dying and coming back seemed to take its toll, but she was strong, and a fighter. Over the next couple of weeks she would prove to be just as much of a fighter as I thought she was. She got stronger and was talking like her regular self. She still couldn't quite walk though. Her feet had Gout, her legs were weak, her bones were deteriorating, and her balance was still off. It was like a baby learning to walk again, but she wasn't going to give up. I wouldn't allow her to give up. About a week or two later she started walking again. Not how you it I would, but slowly, like an infant; but any steps were better than no steps at all. By then she could come out and relax at my house. I would pick her up, cook for her, pray for her. We would have a ball. When it was cold out we cuddle in front of the fireplace with the boys and watch movies. She loved coming to my house. It was a regimen for us, and we couldn't wait for our next Mother/Daughter Day. I just wanted to enjoy her and learn more about.; not to mention I had a few things I need to answers to. I hope my mom wouldn't feel disrespected by my questions, but this conversation was long overdue. So, I had made up in my mind that during my next days off of school and work I would pick her up, cook for her, and we will talk about all the taboo topics she would rather not. That eleven- year-old child still hurts, even though I am now twenty-five years old. I still I need answers so I can heal and move on with my life. I'm sure she also had a few questions for me, and I had a few answers for her as well.

I came to pick my mom up from the rehabilitation center for her visit and of course I was excited to see her but was still nervous. Nervous because the answers I needed weren't going to have us with all smiles. It was going to be a difficult, emotional conversation. I got her to the house where we ate, got comfortable, and I laid across her lap as she rubbed my head. I closed my eyes and just allowed my words to flow.

"Mommy… why did you leave us with those mean people?" Tears began to flow down my face as has my heart started pounding.

"I was introduced to the drug game by my uncle. He gave me dope and I was sniffing at the age of 17. By the age of 18 I was smoking weed and drinking. I got into selling myself just to support my habit. So now I'm on coke, dope, weed, and I'm an alcoholic. The drugs were making my nose bleed, so I graduated and started smoking coke in a glass stem. I felt like I was well off in the streets. I was in too deepen and didn't know what to do as a mother. What I did know was that y'all couldn't be with me in the streets.

I was pretty shocked at some of her answers, but I asked the questions and she gave me the truth.

"I left you with family because I thought you'd be safe. I swear, I didn't even begin to think they would do all the things to you that they did." she cried, referring to my being beaten and whipped with different household items, being molested by relatives as well as the mental and verbal abuse I had to endure. These people really broke me down. "I'm so sorry baby."

"Besides all the drugs, sex, and life in the streets, how was home?" I asked.

"Your grandmother and grandfather worked a lot and were never really around. I was also molested by a family member, which is what led to my drug, sex and alcohol abuse."

Tears of rolled down my face at hearing the information I'd just received. That alone helped me to understand why I ended up the way I did. I needed to understand my mother's upbringing, and for what I heard she didn't have much of a childhood or any real guidance either. I don't think she knew how to truly be a mother because she didn't have one.

"Mom, why didn't you love me as a child? Why didn't you show me attention? You were always so hard on me." I cried.

She leaned forward and wiped away my tears before she answered, "It wasn't that I didn't love you. You were always such an amazing leader who always showed such strong and courage. You never really needed my help. You were and still are my strongest child, mentally and physically. Your brothers and sisters, they needed me. They needed my help more than you did. Falisha got sick and I had to focus on her keeping her alive. She needed me."

Before I knew it I was in my feelings. I even raised my voice a little, but I didn't scream.

"I needed you too Mommy! I was a child trying to be accepted. Trying to understand why mommy hated me so much. Why she never hugged me, kissed me, or tells me she loves me. Yes, I knew Falisha needed you, but I did too. I felt neglected. I felt unwanted. I was just as weak as Falisha. Not physically, but mentally; and I just didn't understand why everybody always loved her more than me. Willy's family, my family… they even loved her more than me. I just felt I didn't even count."

My mother grabbed me close, hugged me tight and kissed me for the first time. I loved smelling her scent. She smelled beautiful. Her heartbeat was strong and in sync with mine. I lifted my head to her chest and just cried as she rubbed my head.

"I am so proud of you. You've grown up so much, and this body is growing tired."

I was an emotional wreck. I kind of brushed off her statement as she kept saying she doesn't have much time. My mom kept wanting to talk about death, and I didn't, but she was trying to prepare me for some things that I would never understand until now. How she still hurts so bad, but she's saved now, so whatever happens she's going to make it to heaven and it's okay.

"Mom, please stop talking like that." I pleaded.

I didn't really want to hear about losing her. I'd just gotten to know her and really gained my mother. Now was not the time.

"I was angry. That's why I used to run away. All the times I was made to feel unwanted and out of place, it felt just like Willies family."

The next thing she said broke my heart, but this had to be talked about. She was upset because she thought I had sex with my stepfather, her husband. I threw up in my mouth. I really felt disrespected, but I need to tell her what I had seen those years back. I was home alone with Garret and my sister Falisha. I saw her kiss him before I went to sleep and had a sneaky sexual interaction.

"I would never do that to you. You're my mother."

"I felt that you wouldn't" she cried.

I went on to let her know it was when she was on parole and she flipped her husband's truck and she ended up in jail, that's when the sexual interaction started. He would always make me look like that bad kid so she could put me out and they could be alone. Everything made more sense now looking back. My mother was disgusted, but she explained she knew and chose to stay with him because she didn't have proof. He also provided for her and my son, even though he wasn't his.

"He was a nasty ass bastard. He was molesting his siblings when they were kids and had a child with his sister that he doesn't even claim. Of course the boy is mentally retarded. If did some nasty shit like that, so I wouldn't put nothing past him."

She told me while I was in prison and when she first started getting sick that he left her high and dry. She tried to stay afloat but started getting high again. She was broken-hearted and ended up getting sucked back into that life. That's why my son was brought back to me. She also apologized for taking the privilege of being a mother away from me. She confessed she'd done that because she felt like she was giving back to me and my siblings for the things she did not do for us. She felt like she needed to do that to redeem herself for some of the choices she'd made as a mother. I personally as a mother would have made some of the same choices, but some I would not have made; and not speaking from that lonely child's heart.

"As a child, I couldn't understand and will never respect her decisions. I would never understand how you chose to neglect me emotionally and abandon me, but as a mother, I respect you. I get it Mommy, but the kid in me will never forgive you."

I cried for about another twenty minutes after we got done talking. I felt relieved, and as if a weight were lifted. I was a whole new woman. I understood my life more than ever now, and I had all my answers. Someone did love me, and that's all that matters. I had spent all those years angry and with hatred in my heart, all because I did not understand her way of thinking and why she thought the way she did. I just assumed and went with that, but now I had all this time to get to know her, the beautiful person that she is - and now she can help me heal. It'll be a slow process, but it can be done.

After our long, sensitive weekend, it was time to take my mom back to the rehabilitation center to finish healing herself. I dropped her off and headed home, but since I was in Bridgeton where my peoples Sean lived, I decided to hit him up see what he was doing.

"What you up to?" I asked.

"Chillin'…about to cook. Why don't you stop by? Matter of fact, can you run me to the store? I got you for gas money."

"It's snowing; but when I get there you can get your ass in this car and you can drive yourself to the store. I'm scared of black ice." I replied and he laughed

"Okay, see you soon."

I pulled up to Sean's house, beeped the horn and ran to the other side of the car, happy to see friend when he came out running. He was about six foot one with dreads and dark skin. Brother had a Sunni, which was salt and pepper, nice full lips, a heart of gold, and he was just on the chubby side. He drove trucks for a living, and he had that money. He wasn't my type, loves himself some me and I knew it, so I kept him around. He always sent me money if I needed it, cooked for me, and always had a gift or two every time he sees me, so I knew he was a keeper. Don't get it twisted, he was fuckin with more drugs and guns than the army. That was because he was Jamaican, and you know they play, so he was my best friend... only he was a guy.

Anyway, he jumps in the car and we take off. He gets to the corner, turns left, and hits the radio to play my Jadakiss CD. This nigga hits a patch of black ice, we spin about three times then crash head on into a fuckin big ass tree. I was knocked out for a good for ten minutes. Good thing I was wearing my seatbelt, or I would have gone through the windshield. I woke up to being tapped on my shoulder and someone asking if I was okay. The airbags had deployed, the front window was broken, and the front end was crumbled up like a piece of paper. The car was smoking, and the alarm was going off. My heart was pounding so fast, my head was spinning, and the lights from the ambulance weren't making it any better. I couldn't believe he just crashed my car. I had just gotten this Lexus. All I could think about was I was glad to be alive, but he will be replacing my fucking car. Shit, he gets money, it shouldn't be that hard.

The cops started asking questions like, "Was he drinking?" "Does he have a license?" "Was he okay?" I had the medical staff in my face, telling me not to move and flashing lights all in my eyes. They helped me out the car, put me on a stretcher and transported me to the nearest local hospital where my son's dad and me. My mom was calling my phone all while this was happening, but I couldn't answer. I just waited to get checked out so I could get on my way home. I was pissed. I just got that damn cat and his big ass crashes my shit. I couldn't wait to leave so I could get my money for my car.

About five hours later my blood test, scans and x-rays came out fine. I had a small contusion, but I was blessed and able to walk away. I got in the car with my kids and Dad, who dropped me off at home. I jumped right on the phone to call Sean so I could let him know how much I paid for my car and insurance.

"I'm sorry. I'mma see what I can do, but at that point I'm broke and don't have it to give you." was his response, and all that did was piss me the fuck off.

"You crashed my car, so you better do what you need to do to replace my shit." He pissed me off as he kept saying what he didn't have, so I said, "You have a few days or I'm showing up at your house snapping." and I hung up on him disgusted and irritated.

I took some pain meds and a shower before I took it down. I just was drained. I still had school and work - and I was back to catching that bus. This was not how I planned things.

I gave Sean a couple days before I called him back again. He told me to stop by his mom's, and they had come up with an idea to get me a new vehicle. I felt like I shouldn't have to talk to his mom because she didn't crash my car, and he was a grown ass man. So why in the hell he got me sitting down with his mother; but I went anyway, and out of respect I'll listen to the old lady. She was really irritating me, but I listened to her. She said that she had been with a dealership for about 10 years, and that's where she bought all her vehicles from. She told me that she could get me a car from there and he would just have to pay the payments on it. I was in agreement because I needed a vehicle and it sounded okay until we paid off the balance for my car, so I jumped on it. We jumped on the bus and me and Sean headed over to the car dealership. When I got there he had the money for my down payment, and the money for my car insurance. I did all the paperwork and ended up with a 2016 Hyundai. It was a nice car. It was purple with ta interior and it drove really nice, so I was satisfied. It wasn't a Lexus, but I wasn't walking either.

After we finished the paperwork we drove off the lot. You know we chopped it up, but I was just disgusted at how I'd just gone from a Lexus to a damn Hyundai Sonata; but a pimp decision had to be made so I wasn't walking to school or work. This car cost me $6,999, which was way more than I paid for my Lexus, and the payments were $270 a month, that I don't make. I have to get it in writing because he was paying, I wasn't, but he had other ideas.

"I'm not paying that note. You're gonna have to make them payments."

"Your Lexus only was 25, so that's what I'm paying."

I went off. "First of all, I didn't have payments bitch. My Lexus was bought straight out, so you can't even compare notes."

He kept trying to go back and forth with me, trying to make it my fault that he crashed my Lexus. He thought he was going to try to sucker me into some payments for my Lexus.

"My car was paid off, now you wanna tell me what you're not going to pay?!" I just went crazy.

He kept trying to talk the same bullshit and I cut him off.

"I mean business. Your ass will be paying more to get your windows in your house fixed than you did my car!"

I think from the tone of my voice and my threats he got the picture. I wasn't playing no games. I worked hard for my stuff. I didn't rob, steal, or kill to get what I had, and I have everything I need. So yeah, he was paying that shit.

Three days later Sean called me and said he had the payment for my car. He knew I wasn't fuckin' playing. It wasn't enough to get me in the car and get me back on the road, and that's all that matters. His mama said he's going to talk to me. I didn't want beef or none of the shenanigans, so I humbly excused myself. I was going about my business to discuss what me and Sean was doing. We went out back and he got this big ass Dutch rolled up. I love the smell, even if I can't smoke. Smelling weed never hurt nobody. We sat, talked, and he pulled about $2,000 out before telling me, "I'll be working on getting the rest." He sold his .45 caliber gun and still had a 4T Tack to sell, so he should have my money soon. Of course people were telling him not to pay for my car. Trying to soup him up to get his ass whooped was what they were doing. I pretty much told him don't play with me. This guy was in his bag and he loved me anyway, so he's trying to tell me how he's been in love with me all these years and are you going to take care of me.

Of course my rude ass said, "Let's work on replacing my car first."

"Cool."

He just wasn't who I see myself with. He was a beautiful soul, he just wasn't for me, but of course he just kept going. He was steady complimenting me, telling me all these things that he would do for me. All I could think about was getting back to what I know: working, school, and family.

I was trying to stay busy, so on my days off I would volunteer at the Family Success Center, where I got into a little facilitating program in town. I was certified to teach parenting classes, life skills and so forth. I thought that was something good to have just because I was excited about the relationships I would form. I met a few people in high places, and I was also asked to speak to over 600 people because my story would touch most survivors in the program. We were asked to tell something about who we are and what we have been through. They felt that my story would change a few people's lives. I definitely was excited. I must say they also experienced some rough times in their lives, but it wasn't shit compared to mine.

I spoke with pain, healing, and mourning in my voice. I spoke from a lonely child's heart. The room fell quiet and tears started flowing. Not mine, but those in the crowd. It wasn't about race or who's story was more important at the time in that moment. I saw white men crying, old white ladies and of course those of color. By the time I was done everyone was hugging me and wiping tears. It was so overwhelming. The questions started flowing. How did you do it? How have you not lost your mind? Then there were those who felt like you're wearing your struggles well, or you don't look like what you've been through. Then out of nowhere this man walks up to me and asks had I ever spoke to big crowds before and if so, would I like to share my story to about 600 people at a conference in New York City. I cried out of joy and I agreed to do it. I was so excited. I went home and started writing. I had to be ready. This was going down in two weeks, I had never spoken to anyone before that program, and certainly not 500 damn people; but shit, I felt like if I can rob, steal and fight, I can give back just as much energy by doing something positive.

I couldn't wait to share the news with my mom and sons. My mom was just as happy as me. She was giving me pointers and ideas. She was all in with me. She even helped me find something more classy for the event, and Lord knows I was going to be cute. Looking all professional stuff; but I tell you what goes up must come down. I was disgusted. The devil was back at it. So, Mom informed me I might not be able to go to this conference because I was on Parole and wasn't allowed to leave the state. My best option to see how it turns out is to call and find out from my parole officer if I was able. Come to find out, I may never exhale or take advantage of certain opportunities. I'll probably never get the chance again to speak in front of so many people, but I did call for one. Of course he denied me. I was not allowed to stay no matter what it was or whoever I was with. I wasn't getting paid for it, so it wasn't considered a job but as volunteer work. I begged him and he just would not let up. I tried to explain to him that it was productive, and I wasn't getting in trouble, but he still denied me. I began crying again. I felt blocked out - thrown to the side. My dreams and hopes again didn't happen, but they ended up going to the conference and it turned out wonderful even though I wasn't able to speak, but all I could do was cry. How was I going to tell the guy that I'm a convict and parole won't let me go? I couldn't, so I just said I felt ill and will speak to him some other time. Hurt, I just had to move on.

I still attended the program and didn't let that stop me. I just wanted to relax, and it was always something. The devil always finds a way to attack me, and I couldn't catch a break, but sleep would just make it easy for the moment. What could I have done that provoked this attack? I would have nothing to say until decided to stick to what I knew. I called Mom and told her we had to hang out this weekend to get my mind off things, and for her to pack up and get ready for Christmas, which was around the corner. I just wanted to enjoy my time with family and make memories. I knew Mom would probably stay out until after Christmas at my place, which I didn't mind. It would be the best Christmas of my life, having her here with my kids, and it was definitely going to be awesome. Not having her be in my life as a child put a hole in my soul - something no one will ever be able to heal. I am a motherless child, so any and every moment I cherish. We had become so close and trying to grow even closer.

No one ever thinks to really go back and do the research on how their parents were raised or how their parents were raised. It influences the way you're raised all the way to the way you raise your children - or your children raised their children. it's up to you to break that cycle, and I did just that. I can't hold my mother accountable for the decisions she has made as an addict. She was an addict who did not understand what it took to be a mother, but she knew what it took to protect me. My mother put me in a home with people she thought I was okay with. People that would keep me safe and no harm would come to me because these people were family. Little did she know, I would've rather been with my addict parents than be in a house where I was not accepted. I was considered the black sheep because I looked nothing like these dark-skinned people. I felt so out of place you know, and my mother never knew what I had gone through; but the moment I sat down and had that conversation with my mom, the healing began. She filled that void when she shared her most intimate thoughts with me, of which I had no understanding beforehand.

As a hurt, lonely child we never go as far as doing our research. We hold on to the resentment and hatred towards our parents for not being there or not acknowledging us - for not giving us the parental guidance and protection we needed, but in all actuality they didn't receive it, so they wouldn't even know where to start. I give props to those parents that they come back and break the cycle – who made an effort to learn. I will always love my mother, but the lonely child in me will never understand her methods. However, I respect it and I always will.

Christmas was here and I was preparing to cook dinner for my family, wrap presents, put up decorations and make memories. I was drained, but I still did my Christmas shopping, decorated my house, and got things in order. My sons helped out by putting up our Christmas tree and decorations. I recorded that and them opening their presents. Christmas definitely was a blast. I couldn't have asked for a better Christmas.

After we opened presents, we ate breakfast and watched movies. I sat next to my mom while trying to rest and she whispered to me, "I'm so tired baby…and I feeling myself getting weaker. This pain is too much to bear - but I'm trying to make sure you ready when I leave."

I realized how much pain she was in and how much it took out of her to fight, but I was being selfish. I didn't want to let her go, but I couldn't stand by and watch her suffer in pain.

"I understand Mom. If want you want is to let go, it's okay. I know it'll be a hard task, but I know now how to explain to the kids that you'll be going to heaven."

Losing my mom will be one of the hardest things I'll have to deal with in this life, so I've been mentally preparing myself for this moment.

"All I ask is that you make sure you siblings are okay." she said weakly.

I'm the middle child and have three siblings older than me that I'm sure are not going to listen to anything I say, but I promised her I would do my best to make sure that they are okay as my heart broke at that moment.

"I couldn't be prouder of you." she said, and those words meant the world to me.

To make her proud of me was all I ever wanted. My only regret was taking so long to ask the hard questions and come to an understanding, all while putting myself in unhealthy situations. I can say that am mentally, emotionally, and physically scarred, but I am not broken. I'm doing things in my life now that I could never imagine, and it's because I have that strength that those precious moments I shared with my mother allowed me to do so.

I have an awesome relationship with my son and I'm thankful for that. I regret that I waited so long to love and understand her.

I went to work and sent the kids off to school as I regularly did. While at work, my cell phone rings, and it was my grandmother calling. She never calls me, so I was kind of leery, but I answered the call.

"Buddha." she said, calling me by my nickname.

"Yes Grandmom?"

"Where are you and the kids?" she asked.

"I'm at work and the kids are at school. What's going on? Is something wrong?" I asked, now worried.

"There's something I need to tell you." she said sadly.

"What is it?" I asked.

"Your mother… she passed away last night in her sleep.

My whole soul cried as I wept, and there was nothing I could do to stop the pain I was in; but what I had over everyone was I was ready. My mom had prepared me for this day so I could be there for my siblings. I could be that strength they needed because she made me strong enough to face this day, but still I was hurt. I think she decided to let go after we talked Christmas when I told her she didn't have to suffer anymore and didn't have to endure the pain. So she ended her fight.

My grandmother went on to assure me that everything was going to be okay you know she was setting up funeral arrangements and we'd be meeting up at the nursing home where my mother was residing to view her body. I immediately left work, went to pick up my kids and left them in the waiting area. I walked into my mother's room and she was lying in her bed lifeless with a peaceful look on her face. She had died in peace, and it didn't look like she struggled at all. She looked as if she was only sleeping. I cried my eyes out as I sat with her, kissed her and just took her in. This is only the second person that I've lost that was dear to me, and I had to ID the body. I was prepared and knew this day was coming, but how prepared can you really be to lose your parent? They got my mother together to remove her from the room and told us to separate all her belongings, which my siblings, grandmother and myself would take. Of course they wanted to take her clothes, jewelry, etc. - but I had something no one could ever take, and that was the time we spent together. The bond we created, and no material things could ever replace the conversations we had. I'm so thankful that I got a chance to experience that with her - to learn who my mother really was, and she was awesome. She was everything.

I am still a lonely child. I'm still a motherless child because I didn't have enough time to spend with her. I feel like I cheated myself out of so much time because we went through so much turmoil that we didn't even get along enough to learn each other way before the time we had just been given. I regret deeply taking so long to love her. To forgive her and to understand her. I just always wanted to tell my story and just get it out there - hoping and praying that one day this would touch somebody somewhere, somehow in some kind of way. My mother was a writer, and I decided to tell our story through this book. What better way to recognize her and to show her appreciation? Even having to deal with so much in my life, I love my mother; and to her I say thank you for helping to heal this lonely child.

Check Out These and Other Hot Reads from Pen
Sistas Publications…Available on Amazon!

Only Death Can Keep Me from Him

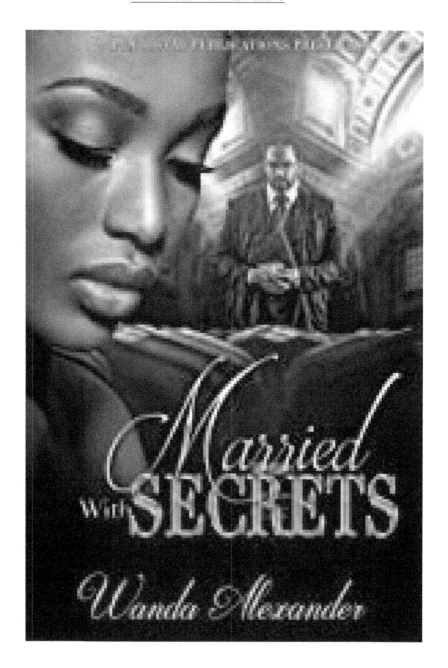

Made in the USA
Middletown, DE
24 September 2020